SterlingHouse Publisher, Inc.   Pittsburgh, PA

Other books by Glenn Ickler:
One Death Too Many
Camping on Deadly Grounds
Stage Fright
Murder by Coffee
A Deadly Calling
Out at Home

MN

A DEADLY VINEYARD

ISBN-10: 1-56315-458-7
ISBN-13: 978-1-56-315458-4
Trade Paperback
© Copyright 2009 Glenn Ickler
All Rights Reserved
Library of Congress #2009922481

Requests for information should be addressed to:
SterlingHouse Publisher, Inc.
3468 Babcock Boulevard
Pittsburgh, PA 15237
info@sterlinghousepublisher.com
www.sterlinghousepublisher.com

Pemberton Mysteries
is an imprint of SterlingHouse Publisher, Inc.

Cover Design: Brandon M. Bittner
Interior Design: Kathleen M. Gall

All rights reserved. No part of this publication may be reproduced, stored in a retrieval system, or transmitted in any form or by any means…electronic, mechanical, photocopy, recording or any other, except for brief quotations in printed reviews…without prior permission of the publisher.

This is a work of fiction. Names, characters, incidents, and places are the product of the author's imagination or are used fictitiously. Any resemblance to actual events or persons, living or dead, is entirely coincidental.

Printed in U.S.A.

ACKNOWLEDGMENTS

Sincere thanks to Sarah Trudel,
Recreation and Interpretation Coordinator,
The Trustees of Reservations—Island Region,
for sharing details of the group's piping plover program.

CHAPTER 1

WHERE'S WALTER?

Announcing that "this is the place," Dave Jerome brushed a drop of sweat off the tip of his nose with the back of his left hand, hauled his suitcase up the steps onto the porch of the sprawling, Victorian-style home and knocked on the front door.

The four of us who had followed Dave for nearly half a mile, schlepping our luggage in the muggy July heat of Martha's Vineyard, traipsed up behind him and waited for the door to open.

A minute went by. No response from within. Dave knocked harder. Another minute went by. Still no one came to the door.

"Are you sure this is your Uncle Walt's cottage?" I asked. In my mind, a cottage was the size of the gingerbread structure where the cannibalistic witch imprisoned Hansel and Gretel. This place looked like a Victorian version of our modern-day McMansions.

"I've been coming to this cottage for 10 years," Dave said. "And Uncle Walt hasn't moved."

Dave had assured me that his uncle would be happy to be our host. I'd begun to wonder about the accuracy of this assessment approximately 20 minutes earlier when his uncle failed to meet us with vehicular transportation at the Martha's Vineyard Steamship Authority ferry landing in Oak Bluffs. Dave had dismissed it as merely a matter of miscommunication. Now there seemed to be a matter of misplacement as well.

Dave had tried to call Uncle Walt while we were on the ferry, but got shuffled to his voicemail. So we dragged our bags (thank heaven for luggage with wheels) through the green expanse of Ocean Park and along a bumpy blacktop street until we reached the porch where we now were standing.

Dave knocked again, pounding with the side of his fist. Maybe Uncle Walt was hard of hearing.

"He knows we're coming, but he hasn't answered my e-mails or returned a phone call for the last week," Dave said. "All I can think of is that he's probably out working on another story. You'd never know the man's retired, he keeps so busy all the time."

Next door, a thin, gray-haired man wearing only shorts and sandals straightened up from weeding his flower bed and walked toward us. "If you're lookin' for Walt, he ain't there," the man said. "Ain't nobody seen him since they found that guy's body about a week ago."

Dave turned toward the neighbor. "Body?" he asked. "What guy's body?"

"That treasure hunter fella that Walt wrote about," the man said. "Big story in the *Boston Globe* when they found his body. Didn't you see it?"

"We're not from this area," Dave said. "I'm Walt's nephew from St. Paul, Minnesota. He's expecting us on the island today." *Us* included Dave's wife, Cindy; my best friend and working companion Alan Jeffrey; his wife, Carol; and me. Oh, and an unhappy 12-pound feline named Sherlock Holmes that I was lugging in a cat carrier.

I'm Warren "Mitch" Mitchell and I work as an investigative reporter for the *St. Paul Daily Dispatch*. Alan Jeffrey is the *Daily Dispatch's* top award-winning photographer and Dave Jerome is the paper's highly creative and extremely popular staff cartoonist.

"Don't know what to tell you folks, except that Walt hides a key under the soap dish in the outdoor shower behind the house," the neighbor said. "That'll get you in."

"Thanks," Dave said. "I'll get it and we can all go in and make ourselves at home." His voice sounded positive, as if everything was fine, but the look in his eyes betrayed him.

As for me, I was ready to turn around and take the next ferry back to the mainland. This was beginning to feel too much like déjà vu. The purpose of my only previous trip to Martha's Vineyard was to write about the search for a man who had disappeared. Al and I found him, but unfortunately, he was dead. A few days later, I nearly joined him in the land of eternal rest.

I swallowed the urge to walk away and stayed with the others waiting for Dave to return with the key. It took him a couple of minutes because of the expanse of this so-called cottage, which was at least 40 feet wide and approximately three times as deep. It stood two stories high, with a three-level turret sprouting from the left front corner. The porch, which stretched completely across the front and wrapped 20 feet around the right side, was furnished with eight white wicker rocking chairs and two round white wicker tables. In true Victorian style, the basic white color scheme was augmented by four shades of lavender and green, adding up to the traditional five colors.

When Dave invited me to join the group going to his uncle's cottage, he promised me a vacation I'd never forget. My aforementioned previous experience had triggered a firm negative reaction to the prospect of spending two weeks on the Vineyard, but I'd finally accepted because I really, really wanted to meet his Uncle Walt.

Walter Jerome was, as the saying goes, a legend in his own time. He'd been editorial page editor of the *Daily Dispatch* for almost 15 years when it was a family-owned, independent newspaper. Walter won a wall full of awards for his biting editorials and witty Sunday columns, and he was respected by public officials and revered by readers throughout Minnesota and western Wisconsin.

One night, soon after the *Daily Dispatch* became the newest link in the chain of a corporation that owned newspapers in a dozen major cities, the publisher, Herbert Riley, and his Minneapolis counterpart were getting shit-faced together at the governor's annual fishing opener. This event was a weekend booze bash hosted by the governor at a northern Minnesota resort every spring to celebrate the opening of the walleye season.

The walleye opener is a religious experience that ranks ahead of Christmas and Easter in the eyes of Minnesota fishermen. Governors of both political parties traditionally have exploited this, using their opening weekend party as a means of schmoozing members of the news media before the final, usually contentious, weeks of the legislative session.

The Minneapolis publisher had been giving Herb Riley a ration of crap about losing his authority as publisher under the new corporate ownership. He'd been teasing Riley about "corporate now calling all the shots."

"That's not the way it is," Riley had said, hoisting his fourth vodka martini. "I have full authority to operate the St. Paul paper any way I see fit."

"Bullshit!" the Minneapolis agitator had said as he tossed down his fifth scotch on the rocks. "I'll bet you a case of Johnny Walker Black against whatever brand of vodka you name that you can't fire Walt Jerome."

"You're on," Riley had said. The next Monday morning, with his hangover still hammering at the back of his skull, Riley summoned Walter Jerome to his office. Before Walter could say good morning, Riley thanked him for his many years of faithful service and told him that he was being replaced by a younger man who would be more in tune with the generation to which the new, more progressive *Daily Dispatch* intended to cater.

Walter was stunned, the readers were shocked and the high mucky-mucks at corporate headquarters in far-away Florida were distracted by the filing of a monopoly complaint against them by the Federal Trade Commission. By the time the bosses at corporate realized that one of their editorial stars was no longer shining in St. Paul, Herb Riley had found his younger editorial page editor, more than a thousand readers had cancelled their subscriptions in protest and Walter Jerome had begun a new editorial career on Martha's Vineyard, where his 95-year-old grandfather owned a weekly newspaper and a vintage Victorian cottage within walking distance of Nantucket Sound.

My hardcore resistance to a second trip to Martha's Vineyard had melted when Dave told me the name of the uncle with whom we'd be staying. "If I can actually meet Walter Jerome, I'll accept your invitation," I had said, despite my gut feeling about returning to the isle of my near demise.

"Of course you'll meet him," Dave had promised. "He'll love talking to a reporter. He's semi-retired, but he still picks up a lot of freelance work. Just last month, he had a piece in *Men's Adventures* magazine about a guy who's hunting for a ship loaded with South American gold that sank somewhere between Martha's Vineyard and Nantucket in the late 1700s."

Now, as four of us stood in front of the legendary editor's locked front door, the odds of chatting with him were looking slim.

"Where do you think he's gone?" I asked as Dave returned from retrieving the hidden key.

"Beats hell out of me," Dave said. "The last e-mail I got from him said he was looking forward to seeing me and Cindy. He sent that a week ago Thursday. The next morning, Friday, I e-mailed back that I was bringing three guests from the paper, but he never answered that one."

"Maybe he was hinting that he wasn't looking forward to entertaining your guests," Al said.

"No, that's not it," Dave said. "He and Aunt Winnie always enjoyed having a houseful of people in the summer, and since she died, Uncle Walt has wanted company even more. Let's go in and see if he left us a note or whatever."

Dave unlocked the door and we filed into a living room that was as big as my entire one-bedroom apartment in St. Paul. The room looked as Victorian as the outside of the cottage, with voluminous curtains on every window, an Oriental rug on the floor, four more white wicker chairs, a white wicker loveseat, an antique Queen Anne sofa and a scattering of lamps with elaborate shades. The only thing that looked out of place was the coffee table, which was topped by a two-foot-wide slab of weathered, rough-hewn wood.

On the coffee table was a copy of *Men's Adventures* magazine, lying open and face down. Dave picked it up and found that it was open to his uncle's story about the treasure ship hunter.

"Look at this—the guy's name is Wade Waters," Dave said. "Is that a perfect name for a diver or what?"

"Great for a guy hunting for liquid assets," I said.

"He sounds all wet to me," Al said.

"Probably made up that name," I said. "You know, kind of a pseudo-swim."

"I'm going to bail out of here if you guys don't dry up," Dave said.

The flow of watery puns was shut off by Cindy' return. She had gone searching for a note in the dining room and the kitchen.

She spread her empty hands, palms up, and shook her head. "Nothing more helpful than an old grocery list on the kitchen counter," she said.

Dave frowned. "I think I'll go talk to that guy next door," he said. "Maybe he can remember if Uncle Walt said anything about going off-island or something."

"We might as well make ourselves at home," Cindy said after Dave went out the door. She flopped into one of the wicker chairs, Carol took a chair beside her and Al settled onto the sofa.

Before I could sit down, a loud note from the cat carrier reminded me that Sherlock Holmes was still cooped up, so I opened the cage and set him free. Sherlock, who has shared my apartment since he adopted me several years ago, looked slowly around the room, took a leisurely stretch and padded off to explore his spacious new surroundings.

I had used frequent flyer miles to purchase a seat for Sherlock in his carrier—no dark, frosty hole in the baggage compartment for my buddy—but getting him into the cabin had been a challenge. In addition to Sherlock's portable shelter, I was carrying my laptop, which I had removed from the luggage I was checking. The people at the security checkpoint had insisted that I could only take one carry-on and I had to show them Sherlock's boarding pass. At the gate, I received the same lecture before I displayed the boarding pass. Onboard, I had to convince a doubting flight attendant that I had paid to have a cat sit beside me.

With Sherlock Holmes free to prowl throughout the cottage, I flopped down next to Al on the sofa and looked at my three companions. All three looked as energetic as Sherlock when he's found a sunny patch of carpet after a heavy meal. And why not? Since rising at 5 a.m., we had traveled halfway across the country by taxi, airplane, bus and ferry, and topped off our day with the sun-baked trek from the pier to the cottage.

The walk in the sun had been particularly rough on fair-haired Carol. Her Nordic skin was pink on every exposed area except her nose, which was red, and her blue eyes had lost their sparkle. Cindy, whose forebears were Italian, had not been scorched by the sun, but her dark curls were hanging in moist strings down to her eyebrows and her expressionless face was glistening with sweat.

Neither Al nor I had acquired a sunburn, but his eyes were closed and his dark-bearded chin was almost touching his chest as he relaxed with his legs straight out in an exhausted slump.

As for me, I felt like a lobster that had been in the boiling pot too long, and I was ready for a nap. I wiped a film of perspiration off my light brown mustache with the back of my hand, leaned back and stretched out to assume the same pose as Al. But at six-foot-one, my legs extended three inches farther than his, and when I straightened them, my feet contacted a newspaper on the floor beneath the coffee table. I reached down, picked up the paper and looked at the front page. It was the previous Friday's *Boston Globe*.

As I perused the page, a three-column headline below the fold not only caught my eye, but caused both of my eyes to open to their full width. The headline said, "Treasure hunter's body found."

The story, datelined Oak Bluffs, began: "An Oak Bluffs fisherman snagged the submerged body of nationally-known treasure hunter Wade Waters in Nantucket Sound, about a mile from Edgartown, shortly before sunset Thursday.

"Waters, 54, had been missing for five days, according to local police. His boat, the All That Glitters, has been based in Oak Bluffs harbor since April, when he began searching for the wreckage of the Daniel French, a sailing vessel believed to have sunk in Nantucket Sound in the late 18th century."

CHAPTER 2

MORGAN AND MANNY

The newspaper story went on to say that the body had been identified by Waters's partner, Charles Morgan, and that an autopsy would be performed to determine the cause of death. I read the story aloud to the group and we were all silently digesting this information when Dave came bounding in the door.

"The guy next door says he has no idea where Uncle Walt might be," Dave said. None of us replied and Dave looked around the room. "Why are you all looking so weird?"

I held up the newspaper, pointed to the headline and gave him a quick summary of the story. "It's like the guy next door said: the treasure hunter's body appeared about the same time your uncle disappeared," I said. "Sort of like a magic act."

"You think finding the body had something to do with Uncle Walt going away somewhere?" Dave asked.

"Probably a coincidence," I said. "But they did have a working relationship. Your uncle had to spend a lot of time with the guy to get enough stuff for a long magazine piece about him."

"This is crazy," Dave said. "I can't imagine there's any connection between finding the body and losing Uncle Walt."

"The neighbor has no clue about your uncle?" Al asked.

"He said the only person who might have some idea of where

he went is his housekeeper," Dave said. "He called her Daffy Dolly and said she rides around Oak Bluffs on a bike and cleans houses and runs errands for people."

Cindy Jerome rose and stared at her husband. "Daffy Dolly?"

"I asked about that name," Dave said. "Apparently her wheels don't have their full complement of spokes, but a lot of people like her and hire her because she does good work."

"So, we're looking for an oddball woman on a bike?" Al asked.

"An oddball woman at least 60 years old on a bike, to be exact," Dave said. "With stringy white hair and a body like a fireplug, according to Mr. Oswald next door. Daffy Dolly's the one we need to talk to."

"Maybe we should also talk to the dead guy's partner," Al said. "What's his name? Morgan something?"

"Charles Morgan," I said. "You're right. He might have seen Walt since the body was found."

"To the harbor we must go," Dave said.

"There's no point in all of us going," Cindy said. "Carol and I should stay here in case Uncle Walt comes back." Cindy managed a household that included two teenage daughters and a 42-year-old husband who spent far more time at his drawing board than helping around the house. She was accustomed to taking charge.

"We'll unpack and put things away while you guys go hunting," said Carol. A junior high English teacher by trade, the wife of a man who often worked odd hours and the mother of a 16-year-old daughter and a 14-year-old son, Carol was equally adept at setting a house in order.

"Good thinking," Dave said. "We'll go check out this Morgan guy and look around for the lady on the bike."

Before leaving, I dug a tray and a small sack of kitty litter out of my bag and prepared a facility for Sherlock Holmes in a corner of the first-floor bathroom. Nothing wears out one's welcome quicker than a cat mess on the rug.

The three of us walked back through Ocean Park, a two-block-wide by one-block-deep expanse of lush green grass dotted with numerous multi-colored flower beds. When we passed the tall gazebo in the center of the park, I felt a chill as I recalled finding a woman I'd planned to meet there slumped in a lawn chair with a bullet hole in her head. Such scenes do not fade easily from the memory.

A subsequent boat ride with the man who'd killed this woman had barged back into my brain the moment I'd boarded the ferry in Woods Hole. The man had murdered two people, and he came within inches (a bullet) and seconds (the deep water) of making me corpse number three.

I'd been thinking about that boat ride all the way across Nantucket Sound, and when I'd walked off the ferry in Oak Bluffs, my face and body had been slick with a coating of cold sweat despite an air temperature of 82 degrees.

"Are you okay?" Dave had asked. "You look as gray as those raw oysters they were selling in the airport restaurant."

"I'm fine," I'd lied. "But being on the water and seeing this island brought back some nasty memories."

"Relax, Mitch," Dave had said. "Nobody's going to try to kill you this time around. The guy who shot you killed himself, didn't he?"

"Yes, he's gone," I'd said. "But the memory of that boat ride lingers on."

"Forget the last time," Al had said. "You know that could never happen to you again."

I began to feel better after we were out of the park and past the Steamship Authority ferry terminal. We continued down a gentle slope to the sheltered harbor, which was too small to accommodate vehicle-carrying ferries the size of the one we'd arrived on. It was late afternoon on Saturday, July 1, and the harbor was clogged with pleasure boats of every make and model imaginable.

We found the All That Glitters tied up about midway between the harbor's entrance and its squared-off inland base. I was surprised to see that the treasure hunter's vessel was no bigger than the one-man commercial fishing boats that I've always thought were too little to venture out onto the ocean. Personally, I prefer a flat-bottomed row boat on a quiet, fresh-water lake.

The All That Glitters was painted a non-glittering black, but the name on the stern was done in gold letters that provided a bright, decorative note. There was no rust showing above the water line, which was a sign of diligent maintenance, and the deck looked clean and uncluttered.

A burly man with whiskers like Blackbeard the Pirate was dozing on a folding lawn chair near the stern. He wore a long-billed fisherman's cap that originally was white but had weathered into various shades of gray, a yellow T-shirt decorated with a toothy cartoon shark pursuing an unsuspecting swimmer and a baggy pair of brown, knee-length shorts. His bare feet were decorated with tufts of hair on top near the base of his toes.

Dave stepped to the edge of the pier opposite the snoozing man. "Charles Morgan?" he asked in a voice loud enough to rouse a corpse.

The man spoke without opening his eyes. "Who wants him?" It was a deep, gravelly voice.

"My name is Dave Jerome. My uncle, Walter Jerome, did a magazine story on your skipper, Wade Waters."

Blackbeard opened his eyes, pushed the bill of the cap back a few inches and looked at us. "Skipper is it?" he said. "Guess you didn't read the story."

"What do you mean?" Dave asked.

"If you did, you'd know that we was partners." The last word was pronounced pahtnahs, with no traces of an *R*. It was obvious that Charles Morgan was a native of New England.

"Sorry," Dave said. "I haven't had a chance to read the piece. I didn't mean to insult you, Mr. Morgan."

"Reckon it's Cap'n Morgan now," he said. "Just like the guy on the bottle of rum. So what brings you here?"

"We're looking for my uncle. His neighbor hasn't seen him since...since they found your partner's body and we thought he might have come by here to, you know, offer his condolences."

The self-commissioned "Cap'n" rose slowly and walked toward us, stopping directly in front of Dave. Morgan appeared to be my height but he carried about 30 more pounds than my 185, mostly in his shoulders, arms and chest. The boat was riding slightly above the dock on high tide, so Morgan towered over Dave, who, like Al, is about three inches shorter than I am.

"'Fraid I can't help you," Morgan said. "I ain't seen the man since he dropped off a copy of the magazine just before my skipper went missin'." There was a clear tinge of sarcasm in the word *skipper*.

"He never talked about going away to do another story or anything?" Dave asked.

"Nope."

"Well, sorry to have bothered you."

"No problem."

"Oh, one more question," Dave said. "Do you know where to find a woman called Daffy Dolly?"

"Nope."

"Okay. We'll be running along then. If my uncle happens to come by, would you tell him we're at his cottage looking for him?"

"Yep." With that, Morgan turned away and went back to his

chair. As he walked away, we saw a foot-long pony tail poking through the opening in the back of his cap. The color matched his beard.

"Nice talking to you," I said before turning to leave. *Cap'n* Morgan's eyes were already closed.

"Well, that was a lot of nothing," Dave said as we started retracing our steps.

"A man of few words," Al said.

"It looks like few ambitions, too," I said. "I wonder what he'll do about the sunken treasure with his partner gone. From what I read in the paper, Waters was clearly the expert."

"Nationally-known treasure hunter," Al said. "I doubt that *Cap'n* Morgan has the smarts to find the sunken ship without him."

"What if they'd already found it before Waters went to dwell with the fishes," Dave said. "That would leave the whole prize to *Cap'n* Morgan."

"Are you suggesting that the new Cap'n might have helped his late partner go overboard?" I asked.

"It wouldn't be the first time somebody was killed for a stack of gold," Dave replied.

"How Waters got into the drink isn't our problem," Al said. "We need to dredge up your uncle."

"He'll appreciate your dry humor when he surfaces," Dave said.

We were back at the Steamship Authority terminal and, as we turned to cross over to Ocean Park, I saw the Oak Bluffs police station just off to our right. "Why don't we talk to the local cops while we're here?" I said.

"Why would we?" Dave asked.

"If your uncle's been missing for a whole week, somebody should report it," I said.

Dave looked skeptical, but finally nodded in agreement. We trekked across the street and walked into the police station where Al and I had spent much of our time during our last Martha's Vineyard excursion. When the desk sergeant asked if he could help us, I asked if Detective Gouveia was available. The sergeant picked up his phone, said a few words and nodded to us. A moment later, Detective Lieutenant Manny Gouveia walked into the lobby.

"Remember us?" I asked, putting an arm around Al's shoulders.

"Oh, my god!" Manny said. "Ain't you the guy the crazy minister tried to kill?"

"That's me," I said. "And you must remember my faithful photographer friend."

"Couldn't forget either one of you," Manny said. "You were both a pain in the ass. Don't tell me you're back here to look for another missin' man."

"We hadn't planned on that but, yes, we are, in fact, looking for another missing man," Al said.

"Are you shittin' me?" Manny asked.

I assured him that we weren't and introduced Dave Jerome, who told Manny about his missing uncle.

"Jeez, I know Walt," Manny said. "I see him at the lunch counter at Linda Jean's a couple of times a week."

"Did you see him at all last week?" Dave asked.

"Come to think of it, no," the detective said. "But I been pretty busy ever since they found that treasure hunter's body. That could be a homicide, you know."

My knee-jerk reporter response kicked in. "What makes you suspect that?"

Manny started to reply, but shut his mouth quickly and shook his head before responding. "Oh, no," he said. "I ain't sayin' nothin' to no reporters."

"I'm here on vacation," I said. "I'm not writing a story."

"You guys ain't never on vacation," Manny said. "Now, what's the scoop on Walt?"

Dave explained that Walt's neighbor hadn't seen him for a week and that Walt hadn't responded to his e-mails or returned his phone calls since the previous Friday.

"Hey, didn't he do some kind of a magazine story about the treasure hunter?" Manny asked. Dave replied that he did.

"Yeah," Manny said. "Come to think of it, the chief needs to talk to Walt about that."

"Why?" Dave asked.

"Routine. The chief needs to talk to everybody who had contact with the dead guy close to the time he disappeared. But you're tellin' me that Walt's disappeared, too?"

"Yes, I am," Dave said.

"So, are you here to file a missin' person report?"

"Well, yeah, I guess that would be a good idea."

"Okay. The sergeant's got the form you need right there at his desk. We'll get the word out to the guys on the street and let you know when we find your uncle." Manny turned toward the door leading to his office and looked back over his shoulder. "Nice seein' you two clowns on the Vineyard again—even if you and your buddy did bring us some more work."

"Just one more question," I said. "Do you know where we might find a woman called Daffy Dolly?"

He spun to face us again. "Why in hell would you want to find her?"

"Apparently she does house cleaning and grocery shopping for Walt Jerome," I said.

"Take my word," Manny said. "You guys don't want to find Daffy Dolly." He turned and disappeared through the door.

CHAPTER 3

ON THE JOB

Back at the cottage, we learned that Walt Jerome had not come home and that Sherlock Holmes had chosen a resting place in a back bedroom on the second floor. This room became mine by default so I hauled my bag and my laptop up the stairs.

As I laid the computer on the bed, it occurred to me that I should notify the folks at the *Daily Dispatch* of their former editorial page editor's mysterious disappearance. The missing person report would be picked up by the local police reporters and, because of Walt's status, it might get national distribution through the wire services. I would not want to hear City Editor Don O'Rourke's reaction if he learned of Walt Jerome's disappearance by reading an Associated Press story, especially with Don knowing that three members of his staff were on Martha's Vineyard.

I dug out my cell phone and called the city desk. Because it was after 3 p.m. on Saturday, Gordon Holmberg, the Sunday city editor, was in Don's chair. Gordon's response was exactly what I feared it would be.

"E-mail us a story right away," he said. "Give us some background on what Walt's been doing out there and I'll pump it up by having somebody dig out his bio on this end."

I was no longer on vacation.

About 20 minutes later, as I was tapping away on the laptop, Al appeared in the doorway. "We're heading out for supper," he said. "What the hell are you doing?"

I told him that I'd done my duty and called the paper, and had been given an assignment. I suggested that Al shoot some photos of Walt's cottage to accompany my story. Al groaned and said he would. "How long until you're done with your story?" he asked. "Everybody's ready to hunt up some food."

"Give me another five minutes," I said. "You can shoot some quick pix and be ready to download them as soon as I'm done."

"Another damn working vacation," he said. "How come you always get us into these things?"

"Would you rather have Don read about Walt Jerome's disappearance in the Minneapolis paper?"

"Now you're talking about a nuclear bomb going off."

"Right. Don would unleash a mushroom cloud."

"He's such a fun guy."

"Shitake happens," I said. For once, I got the last word as Al groaned and went to get his camera.

We ate at Linda Jean's, a reasonably-priced restaurant that served excellent food on Circuit Avenue, the main business street in downtown Oak Bluffs. Discovering this haven, which was where the locals hung out, had been the only bright spot in Al's and my previous visit to the Vineyard.

Unfortunately, other non-locals had also found this restaurant and we were forced to wait 25 minutes to get seated. The receptionist handed Dave a buzzer so we could stand outside and watch the tourists saunter by. It was T-shirt and shorts season, and we observed that the majority of the passersby were carrying too much flab and leaving much too much of it exposed to public view.

"Looks like the old-time whaling days are back," Al muttered, nodding toward an almost perfectly round woman whose bulging bare belly hung out over a pair of shorts that were sucked tightly up into her crotch.

"This gives new meaning to being in fat city," I said.

"You guys are awful," said Carol, who, despite having borne two children, has a waist so slender that I could almost get my hands around it.

"But for the grace of God and Weight Watchers, there goes me," Cindy said. She is the same height as Carol but she carries about 15 more pounds, most of it around her tummy and hips.

Before returning to Walt Jerome's cottage, we took a short stroll on the sidewalk above the Oak Bluffs town beach. Al and I described the mess we'd seen on that beach during our previous visit following a raging wind-and-rain storm known in New England as a "nor'easter." Rocks the size of a kitchen stove had been washed up onto the sand. The lifeguard towers had been knocked over and slammed against the bluff. Seaweed had been spread over everything. And, of course, there was the water-logged corpse that Al had spied half-covered in seaweed and lodged in the rocks near the ferry terminal.

Back at the cottage, Dave stuck his head in the front door and called out his uncle's name. We weren't surprised when he got no answer. We all flopped into chairs on the porch and in silence watched the sky grow darker.

Cindy was the first to speak. "It's been a long day and I'm pooped. See you in the morning." She rose and went into the cottage to a chorus of good-nights.

"Sounds good to me," Dave said. He got up and followed his wife.

Carol was the next one to rise. "Me, too," she said. "There's something about flying that wears you out."

"It's from having to flap your arms all the time," Al said.

"That joke is older than the crackers they gave us on the plane," I said.

"Some people collect antique furniture; I collect antique jokes." He stood up and followed Carol through the door.

I sat alone for a few minutes, basking in a cool ocean breeze that ushered in the evening. After my eyes had closed involuntarily several times, I decided it was time to pack it in. Thinking it might be helpful to read Walt's story about Wade Waters and his search for the sunken treasure, I grabbed the coffee table copy of *Men's Adventures* as I passed through the living room and took the magazine with me to my bedroom. True to form, Sherlock Holmes was asleep in the middle of the bed.

I contemplated making a phone call to the most beautiful woman in my life, Martha Todd, who was fulfilling a law school scholarship contract by working for the attorney general of Cape Verde. However, it was an hour past midnight in that island nation, so instead of calling, I tapped out an e-mail message that she could read in the morning.

Communicating with Martha was, by the way, my main reason for bringing the laptop along on vacation. The other reason was that a writer never knows when a story might pop up, as one already had. After sending the message to Martha and deleting a couple of offers for the enhancement of a portion of my anatomy that I believed was already of adequate dimensions, I turned to the magazine article.

In the story, Wade Waters really was quoted as calling Charles Morgan his partner. However, as I read on, I wondered about the equality of this partnership. Waters had the training, the experience and the boat. Morgan had the muscle, but he was a newcomer to treasure hunting, having joined Waters in April when a previous partner quit to take another job. The story didn't say why the other man left or where he went for his new job, which left me wondering about the circumstances of his departure. Had the split up been peaceful or acrimonious? If Waters had been the victim of foul play, here was another man with a possible motive for mayhem.

★ ★ ★

On Sunday morning, I was awakened by a small, warm nose pressing against mine. It was after 9:00 and Sherlock Holmes wanted breakfast. Wondering why I'd been so weak-willed as to bring Sherlock along when I could have left him with my 89-year-old neighbor, Mrs. Peterson, I picked him up, carried him down to the kitchen and spooned some of the food I'd brought along into his dish. I'd have to make a run to the grocery store on Circuit Avenue Monday to lay in a supply for the rest of the week.

Thanks to Sherlock, I was the first one dressed and ready to look for breakfast. It was almost 11 before all five of us were prepared to leave the cottage. I believe the standard description of our preparatory gyrations is "herding cats." We wandered back to the main street, Circuit Avenue, and found a mob milling around outside Linda Jean's. We went across the street and bought take-out muffins, doughnuts and coffee at a bakery, which had an equally-long but faster-moving line. We sat on park benches and ate our brunch in the sun in an open area known as David M. Healey Square.

When he'd finished his blueberry muffin, Al brushed a crumb from his dark mustache. "Okay, now what?" he asked.

"Good question," Dave said, checking his blond mustache and finding it devoid of doughnut debris. "I thought we'd be exploring the island in Uncle Walt's Landrover." Reflexively, I ran the back of my hand across my sand-colored mustache and encountered a bit of blueberry.

"Why don't we take the Landrover?" Cindy asked. "Can't you find the keys?"

"I can't find the Landrover," Dave said. "He always parked it beside the cottage and it's obviously not there."

"So, we're missing a van as well as a man," I said.

"Now the reporter's a lousy poet," Dave said.

"It could be verse," Al said.

"My poetic license stanza lone," I said.

"More likely your poetic license stands expired," said Al.

"Why don't we all stand together and go do something fun?" Carol said. "We could take a walk around Oak Bluffs or catch a bus to another town."

"I saw a place by the harbor where we could rent some bikes," Dave said. "Biking to Edgartown would give us some exercise after sitting at the airport and on the plane all day yesterday."

Renting bikes was the unanimous choice. We traipsed down Circuit Avenue to the rental place, zigzagging around window shoppers all the way. The rates encouraged rentals by the week, so we picked out five bikes with sturdy tires to keep until the following Saturday, with an option to renew them for the second week if we so desired.

As I tried out the bike I'd chosen, I circled near the pier and saw two men on the deck of the All That Glitters. The tall, burly one was easily recognizable as Charles "Cap'n" Morgan. When the shorter, paunchy man turned my way, I saw that it was Detective Lieutenant Manny Gouveia. Oh, to have been a fly on the treasure boat bulkhead.

We rode leisurely to Edgartown on a bike path swarming with weekend riders, stopping occasionally to rest and look at the endless stretch of beach on our left and the long, shallow pond on our right. One of our stops was at a bridge over a narrow opening between the pond and the ocean where youngsters were jumping off the railing into the fast-moving tidal current. Dave, a lifelong movie buff, informed us that several scenes from "Jaws" had been filmed at this spot, although the bridge had been rebuilt since then.

In Edgartown, we ate an early dinner in a restaurant on the harbor and briefly perused the shopping area. The women were astounded by and enamored of the fashions in the dress shops and the men were merely astounded by the prices.

We returned to the cottage in time for me to make my ritual Sunday phone call to my mother and my grandmother, who live together on the family farm in Harmony, Minnesota. Since my father's fatal heart attack 30 years ago, Mom has rented the cropland and the outbuildings to neighboring farmers while continuing to occupy the house and garage.

My hope was that Grandma Goodrich, or Grandma Goodie as she is known, had gone to bed early so I wouldn't have to listen to her ritual lecture on my church attendance, which, for years, had been nil. No such luck. Grandma Goodie answered the phone and as soon as she heard my voice she asked the customary question: "Did you go to church today, Warnie baby?" Just 11 days before my 40th birthday, I was still a mere baby to her.

I gave my usual answer: "Not today, Grandma." But I had a new excuse. "I'm on vacation with a group of people and none of us made it to church."

"You couldn't make your own individual decision to take care of your own individual soul?" she asked.

"I had to go where the car was going." That fictitious excuse sounded weak even to me, but it was the best I could do.

"I suppose you'd have ridden along if the devil was driving and the car was going straight to hell."

"The devil's not allowed on Martha's Vineyard," I said. "And you can't get to hell from here."

"You can make all the silly jokes you want, but the time will come when you'll regret neglecting your soul, Warnie baby. None of us lives forever."

I agreed and promised, as always, to do better in the future. After another warning about the unalterable approach of judgment day, Grandma Goodie passed the phone to Mom. We talked about such things as the comparative weather between Martha's Vineyard and Harmony, the state of the southeastern Minnesota corn crop, the beauty of the ocean here in Oak Bluffs and the fate of the Minnesota Twins, who were second only to God and family in Grandma Goodie's heart but fourth in the American League Central Division.

When I signed off, it was time to feed Sherlock Holmes his supper, for which he obviously had been waiting. Cindy Jerome was in the kitchen looking for a tea bag while I was filling Sherlock's dish. "That's strange," she said.

"What's strange?" I asked.

"The old grocery list that was on the counter is gone. Did you throw it away?"

"No," I said. "Probably Carol. She's the resident neatnik." Carol liked things to be in their proper place, although she wasn't fanatical about it. "Oh, speak of the devil," I said as Carol walked into the kitchen.

"I don't know if it was the devil or an angel, but somebody cleaned up the bathroom while we were gone," she said. "Do you suppose Dave's uncle dropped in?"

CHAPTER 4

HOT PURSUIT

We checked all four bedrooms—three upstairs and one downstairs—and the side sleeping porch to see if Walt Jerome was sacked out somewhere, but he was not in the cottage. When I reached my room, I discovered that the bed I had left in a heap was neatly arranged, tucked and covered with its spread. Somehow, I doubted that Sherlock Holmes had done all this.

"Spooky," Al said when I reported the bed making phenomenon.

"Or daffy?" Dave said. "As in Daffy Dolly?"

"You think she was here?" I asked.

"Who else?" Dave said. "Mr. Oswald said she's my uncle's housekeeper. Maybe Sunday is the day she cleans."

"And we missed her," Cindy said.

"Damn!" Al said. "It could be next Sunday before she comes back and we could still be looking for your uncle."

"We'll catch up with Dolly before that," Dave said. "We've got to find out if she knows where Uncle Walt is. If he's anywhere on the island, we can't live in his house for two whole weeks and never see him."

We agreed that we'd give high priority to the hunt for Daffy Dolly in the morning and went off to our respective bedrooms. I booted up my laptop, opened my e-mail and found a return message from Martha. She'd spent the afternoon at a beach party with a bunch of people from her office and hoped I was overcoming my bad feelings about the Vineyard. My feeling at that moment was envy—envy of the guys from her office who'd had the pleasure of looking at Martha's divine body in a swim suit all afternoon.

I sent back an e-mail briefly describing the activities of our lazy, laid-back day, and signed it with the usual number of kisses and hugs. Before going to sleep, I finished reading the magazine story about Wade Waters and learned that he was competing with another team of treasure hunters in the search for the ship they believed was on the ocean bottom between the Vineyard and Nantucket. The other team, in a boat called Bottoms Up, was operating out of Vineyard Haven harbor, just three miles west of Oak Bluffs. It struck me that the Bottoms Up would be operated by men who wouldn't be unhappy to see Wade Waters dead. My suspicious reporter's mind, and all that.

In the morning, I scraped the last cat food out of the can and decided to replenish my supply before we began our search for Daffy Dolly and Walt. I found Dave sipping coffee and watching the world go by from one of the wicker chairs on the front porch. I told him that I'd be back in a few minutes, got on my bike and rode to the parking lot behind a grocery store called the Reliable Market, which faces Circuit Avenue. As I was about to lock my bike to a railing, a short, stocky woman with stringy white hair came out of the store with a full plastic bag in each hand. She hung a bag on each side of a rack on the rear fender of a beat-up men's bicycle, got on the bike and pedaled away.

This had to be Daffy Dolly. I stuffed the lock back into the pouch on my handlebars and took off in pursuit. She was wearing a white T-shirt and faded yellow shorts that revealed two muscular legs that could have been attached to someone a couple of decades younger, and she was moving damn fast for a 60-something woman on a vintage bike.

My first thought had been to catch Dolly and confront her, but I quickly learned that I could barely keep pace with her. I had the advantages of youth, size and a better bike, but I also had stiff leg muscles and a sore butt from the previous day's ride. Dolly swung up onto Ocean Avenue and turned east—going, as the islanders say, down island—at an amazing speed.

Soon we were whizzing along the same bike path the five of us had ridden to Edgartown on Sunday, but without any traffic to slow Dolly down. I decided to call Al and tell him I was in hot pursuit of Daffy Dolly, but when I reached into my pocket for my cell phone I discovered that I'd left it on the dresser. Sherlock Holmes could call out for a can of tuna, but I was on my own.

As I crossed the first small bridge on this route, I could see that the waters of Nantucket Sound, on the far side of the road, were being rippled gently by a light sea breeze. In the tidal pond on my right, people were digging for clams in motionless, waist-deep water. Again, the sky was an unbroken expanse of blue and the morning sun was warming the air so that even in shorts and a T-shirt my body was beginning to sweat.

By the time we reached the second bridge, where Dave had told us that scenes from "Jaws" were filmed, a waterfall was running off my forehead, irritating my eyes and dripping off my nose onto the handlebars. Still Daffy Dolly pedaled on, apparently unaffected by the rising temperature.

We reached an area at the edge of Edgartown known as the triangle, where the road we'd been following joined Edgartown-Vineyard Haven Road at about a 45-degree angle. The bike path crossed this road and turned left toward downtown Edgartown. Dolly zipped across without stopping and I almost lost her when a couple of aggressive SUV drivers made me wait to follow. With my thigh muscles straining and complaining, I increased my speed enough to narrow the gap between us as we rolled toward the center of Edgartown.

"Please let her stop soon," I said to myself as I got close enough to reduce my speed. My upper leg muscles were burning, my butt was aching and the friction of my shorts against my inner thighs was producing a new sensation of soreness on the tender skin covering that portion of my anatomy. Still Daffy Dolly pedaled on.

Two questions came to mind: (1) Where the hell was this single-minded woman going? (2) Did she know I was following her? If the answer to the second question was "yes," a third question could arise: Would she try to ditch me? And that led to a fourth question: What the hell did I care?

At this point, my physical pain had grown so intense that I put my mental processes on hold and concentrated solely on keeping Dolly in sight. She swung left, passing a sign that read "Chappy Ferry bicycles only." I followed, hoping against hope that we weren't going to board the ferry that would take us to Chappaquiddick. A few minutes later, I learned that we were.

I followed Dolly down the hill to the ferry landing, passing a line of cars waiting for transportation. The On Time Ferry, so named because it had no published schedule and therefore was always on time, was disgorging its cargo of two SUVs, a pickup truck, four bicycle riders and five pedestrians. The barge-like boat was shaped the same on both ends and never turned around, so that what had been the stern on the way to Edgartown would be the bow on the crossing to Chappaquiddick. The On Time Ferry could carry a maximum of three vehicles parked end-to-end, along with numerous bikers and foot passengers.

Dolly dismounted, wheeled her bike onto the ferry and went

all the way to what would soon become the bow. I followed, stopping immediately in the stern in order to stay out of her sight. The On Time Ferry was not where I wanted to confront the woman and quiz her about her destination.

A gray-haired woman in a gray T-shirt, grease-spotted khaki shorts and a faded Boston Red Sox cap asked me for $8. In return, she gave me a ticket, said it was for a round trip and warned me not to lose it. I tucked it into the pocket that should have been holding my cell phone.

Dolly never looked back as the ferry roared across the narrow stretch of water between the Edgartown slip and the landing at Chappaquiddick. Looking at a map the previous day, we'd learned that Chappy was virtually an island unto itself. It could only be reached on the harbor end by riding the On Time Ferry. On the other end, the only access was a narrow spit of sand that required the use of a four-wheel-drive vehicle.

Approximately three minutes after leaving the slip, we hit the Chappy landing with a thud. The gray-haired woman dropped the restraining chain and Dolly took off at her usual speed. I'd welcomed the brief respite on the ferry, but my assorted agonies returned quickly when I got back on the bike and set off behind her.

There was no bike path now, just a two-lane, black-top road that we shared with passing vehicles, most of which were bulky SUVs. Again I wondered how far the woman could possibly be going. Still Daffy Dolly pedaled on and the sun and the temperature both continued their inexorable rise.

About a half-mile from the ferry landing, we passed a row of tent-like beach cabanas with bright red-white-and-blue-striped roofs. I thought there was something familiar about them but where would I have seen them? After all, I'd never been on Chappaquiddick before.

After passing a small pond, there was little to see beside the road. There were mailboxes and driveways, but the houses were hidden behind thick groves of oak and evergreen trees. This stretch of sameness suddenly was broken by a truly ugly junkyard on the left, and shortly after that, the blacktop took a sharp right. Straight ahead was a gravel road, and I was glad to see Daffy Dolly make the turn that kept us on the blacktop.

We'd gone three miles or more when we reached another turn, this one sharp to the left. At the corner was a large rock bearing the carved message "Blow Your Bugle." What the hell was that all about, I wondered as I followed my leader around the turn.

I was in a state of physical meltdown when Daffy Dolly suddenly veered off the blacktop onto a sand and gravel road on the right that made pedaling even more painful. This road was only a single lane wide and it wound through an assortment of evergreens, oaks and scrub oaks. The gravel began to disappear and the wheels of my bike sank deeper as the surface got even softer. My legs were turning to jelly and I was losing ground on Daffy Dolly when she stopped, slid off the seat and began walking her bike.

"Thank God," I said out loud as I abandoned the seat of my pain and started to push my two-wheeled torture chamber.

"Don't thank her too soon," said a male voice behind me. "Drop the bike and put your hands up as high as you can reach."

I stopped and looked back over my shoulder to see who'd spoken. He was tall, rail-thin, deeply-tanned and naked except for a pair of faded blue jeans cut off as short as decency would allow. Most importantly, he was pointing a very large shotgun at my ass.

CHAPTER 5

PRISON CAMP

Obediently I dropped the bike onto the sand and raised my hands toward the sky.

"Walk over to that tree and put both hands on it and spread your feet apart," the man said, gesturing with the gun barrel toward a large oak. "Put your head against the tree, too."

Again I obeyed, assuming the position that I'd seen when bad guys on the TV crime shows were frisked. Seconds later, it was me being frisked, with the man's left hand slapping at my hips, butt and inner thighs as if there were a place to hide a weapon in my shorts. I knew the shotgun was still in his right hand and for a moment I considered making a move to grab it. As if he'd read my mind, the man slapped the side of my face.

"Don't move from that position," he said. "Keep looking straight at that tree, and tell me who you are and why you're following Dolly."

"My name is Warren Mitchell, better known as Mitch, and I'm following Dolly because I thought she might lead me to a man I'm looking for," I said. "Who are you?"

"Who is this man you're looking for?" he said, ignoring my question.

"He's the uncle of a friend. We're staying in his house in Oak

Bluffs."

"Does this uncle of a friend have a name?"

"His name is Walter Jerome."

"And what's your friend's name that you're staying with?"

"Dave Jerome. We're visiting from Minnesota."

The man grunted. "Come away from the tree, pick up your bike and walk straight ahead with it."

Once again, I obeyed. He followed, with the gun still pointing at my ass. When we came to a footpath on the left a minute later, he ordered me to take it. A hundred feet ahead of me, I saw Daffy Dolly standing beside an olive drab Landrover that was generously decorated with rust. The Landrover looked old enough to have been the one used in the filming of *The Gods Must be Crazy*.

Daffy Dolly had taken the grocery bags off her bike and was putting them into the Landrover through the door on the driver side. The vehicle was parked at the very edge of the wooded area, with a broad expanse of sand beyond it. On top of the Landrover, I saw part of a camouflage-pattern tarp that was held in place by a row of rocks. Apparently, this tarp hung down to the ground and covered the side that was away from the trees.

"Sit in that chair," the man with the shotgun said. It was a folding lawn chair that had seen far better days. The metal parts were pitted with rust and the plastic webbing was frayed.

Gingerly, hoping the chair wouldn't collapse under my weight, I sat. Facing the man at last, I was able to view him in more detail. He was barefoot, bearded and bald except for a two-inch, white fringe that circled his head just above the ears. I also noticed that his hands were very steady on the shotgun.

"Dolly, come over here and look at this man," he said, without taking his eyes off me. Dolly walked over and stared at me with watery, pale blue eyes. Her round, leathery face showed no emotion. "Ever see him before?" the man asked.

Dolly's face remained expressionless as she shook her head.

"You've never seen him anywhere in Oak Bluffs?"

Another negative shake.

"I've got ID that proves who I am and where I work," I said. "I'm a newspaper reporter in St. Paul. I've got a press card."

"Let's see it," he said.

I took out my wallet and started to hunt through the cards. "Give me the billfold," the man said. I hesitated and he raised the barrel of the shotgun in a most persuasive manner. I handed him the wallet, wondering if I'd get all of its contents back.

The man looked at my driver's license and the press card issued by the St. Paul Police Department. "You say you're a reporter?"

"That's right," I said.

"What about this friend—this Dave Jerome? What does he do?"

"He's our editorial cartoonist."

"Why are you looking for Walter Jerome?"

"His nephew wants to see him. Dave and his wife and three of us that they brought along as guests are staying in Walter's house. We all want to see him, but he's been missing for a week."

"Have the cops in Oak Bluffs been looking for Walter Jerome?"

"They are now. Dave reported him missing Saturday."

"Shit!" the man said. "What the hell did he do that for?"

The light that had been slowly coming on in my brain flashed at a full 100 watts. "You're Walter Jerome, aren't you?" I said.

"So, what if I am?" he asked.

"You should come home. Your nephew wants to see you."

"It's not that simple."

"Why not?"

"It's a long story."

"I've got plenty of time. In fact, it might be a couple of days before I can get on that bike again."

Walt Jerome smiled and tossed my wallet at me. "Dolly wear you out?"

I nodded. "She can really move on that thing. My riding muscles aren't in that great a shape."

"Like the old prostitute said, life is tough when you pedal your ass."

"That's the seat of my problem all right. But anyhow, tell me what you're doing out here?"

Walt ejected a shell from the shotgun and put the shell and the weapon into the back of the Landrover. He tossed me a 20-ounce bottle of water, which I drained to the halfway point without stopping, and leaned against the vehicle for a couple of minutes while he considered how much to tell me. While he pondered, I scanned the area and saw a small camping stove, some cooking utensils and a coffee pot on the ground.

"I'm killing two birds with one stone," Walt said when he finally spoke. "I'm staying out of sight of whoever murdered a man I wrote a magazine story about and I'm protecting an endangered shorebird."

"The man would be Wade Waters?" I asked.

"That's right. You know about Wade?"

"We read the story in the *Globe* about his body being found. By the way, the cops want to talk to everybody who had contact with him, which includes you."

"That's another reason I can't go home," Walt said.

"Why don't you want to talk to them?" I asked.

"I have my reasons. Next to the killer, I might be the last person who saw Wade Waters alive."

"But if you didn't kill him, why not talk to the cops?"

"Because of circumstances, they might not believe what I'd tell them."

"What circumstances?"

"You ask too damn many questions, Mr. Reporter. Let's just leave it that I'd rather not talk to Chief Forbush or any of his stooges until the killer is caught."

"Okay," I said. "Then tell me why you're hiding from the killer."

"Because he probably thinks I can testify against him, which makes me the next candidate for a deepwater dunking."

"Are you saying that you know who the killer is?"

"I'm not sure, but the killer might think I do. So, I'm a hell of a lot safer here than in Oak Bluffs."

"Okay, that makes sense. But what about your other reason for hiding out here? You said something about protecting some kind of shore bird?"

"You ever hear of the piping plover?" Walt asked. I shook my head and he explained that the piping plover is an endangered species of shore bird that nests in the sand on a beach that's popular with Chappy fishermen. "Come over here, I'll show you where I'm talking about."

Walt led me past the Landrover and out of the trees onto a wide expanse of open sand that sloped gently toward the south. He pointed toward what I took to be a large saltwater pond. "What looks like a pond actually opens into Edgartown harbor on the north end and is called Katama Bay," he said. "You can't see it from here, but there's a little strip of sand at the south end of Katama Bay that separates it from the open waters of the Atlantic Ocean. Fishermen with four-wheelers use that little strip of sand between the bay and the ocean to get to their favorite spots on Norton Point and a conservation area called Wasque Reservation. Sometimes that strip is broken by a storm and it takes months or years for the ocean to deposit enough sand to rebuild it."

"And these fishermen hurt the birds?" I asked.

"Not as much as they used to, but once in awhile you get somebody who either doesn't see too good or doesn't give a shit. The problem is that the plovers are little brown birds that just scrape out a shallow depression in the sand to make a place to lay their eggs. The Trustees of Reservations, which is one of the oldest and best conservation organizations around, tries to protect them, but it's tough because the birds pick their nesting spots at random and they can be hatching eggs and raising chicks anywhere from April to August.

"Every spring, the Trustees stake out the prime nesting spots with marine roping and metal posts, and put up signs saying the area is closed for shorebird nesting of rare species. But the birds sometimes have ideas of their own, depending on the tides, the habitat and the weather. They keep the Trustees people hopping, trying to secure the nesting sites with what they call 'exclosures.'"

"Exclosures?" I asked.

"They make a 6-foot-diameter circle around the nest by putting up a 3-to-4-foot metal fence covered over the top with a fine plastic netting. They decorate this with more metal roping and more signs that tell people to stay away, both with their four-wheelers and their feet."

"And still people harass them?"

"Once in awhile, you get a guy who's pissed about being kept off his pet parking spot. Or you get somebody running over a nest that hasn't been staked out. The Trustees people do a great job of keeping the birds safe during the daytime, but they can't hang around all night. That's where people like me and a couple of my friends come in."

"You patrol the bird sanctuary at night?"

"Exactly."

"So, what do you do to protect the birds?" I asked.

Walt motioned for me to follow him back to the Landrover. He reached into the glove box and brought out a tiny metal object. "You know what this is?" he asked. I confessed that I did not.

"It's a valve core tool. At night, I drive down across the sand and park near Norton Point Beach. When one of these assholes comes in and damages an exclosure or parks too close to a nest, I sneak up, slap a *Save the Piping Plover* sticker on the driver-side window and remove the valve cores from two of the tires. If they've got a spare they can replace one of them, but they've still got one that's completely flat and it's a real bitch steering in the sand that way. Sometimes it chews up the tire that's flat and gets the wheel all full of sand. Anyhow, they usually don't come back."

"You've never been caught by one of those fishermen?" I asked.

"Not yet, knock on wood," he said, tapping the glossy skin on the top of his head with his knuckles. "I've been camping out here to help the plovers for a few weeks during the nesting season every summer since I retired three years ago, sleeping in that backpacking tent over there." He pointed to a tiny, green tent barely visible through the brush.

"So that's how Dolly knew where you were."

"Right. She's been hauling food and water out here for me every summer."

"And she never tells anybody where you are?"

"Dolly won't talk."

"You mean she can't talk?" I asked.

"Oh, no; Dolly can talk all right," Walt said. "But she only does it when she thinks it's really necessary."

"Is that why they call her daffy?" I asked in a softer voice. Dolly was sitting on the ground about 10 yards away with her back against a tree, munching on an apple.

Walt leaned close to me and answered in almost a whisper. "She was brain damaged at birth, but she's smart enough to get jobs cleaning houses and running errands. She lives in whatever customer's cottage is empty at the time. She probably was living in mine when Dave and all you guys moved in."

"I'm sure she's welcome to come back. We're only using the three upstairs bedrooms."

"Dolly never stays where there are people."

Discussing Dave and the cottage brought my attention back to the basic problem of getting nephew and uncle together. With Walt unwilling to return to Oak Bluffs, Dave would have to come to Chappy. I said as much to Walt, ending with my concern about the length of the bike ride. I didn't think Dave's legs and butt were in any better condition than mine.

"There is an easier way," Walt said. "A friend of mine leaves his car keys with me for a month every summer when he goes to visit his daughter in Alaska. Wants me to start it and drive it once a week to keep the battery and tires in shape. I'm not doing it much good right now, but you guys could have a car to use and be performing a service at the same time."

"Sounds a hell of a lot better than biking all the way out here," I said.

"The keys are hanging by the back door and I can tell you where to find the car. It's only two blocks away from my place."

While Walt was writing the address and drawing a map on a scrap of paper, Daffy Dolly stood up, picked up her bike and muttered "goodbye." Walt asked her to wait, went to the back of the Landrover and picked up another piece of paper, which he handed to the woman.

"Next week's list of provisions," he said as Dolly disappeared down the path.

I started to rise from the chair to take the paper Walt was holding out to me, pressing down hard on the metal arms as I dragged my torso upright and straightened my aching legs. There was a scraping, tearing sound as the arms collapsed and the seat fell away behind me. I followed the wreckage to the ground, landing on the part of me that had been tortured and tenderized by the bicycle seat.

When Walt finished laughing—and I finished moaning—he helped me to my feet. I apologized for wrecking his chair, which provoked more laughter, and said I'd bring Dave to see him soon, maybe even later today.

"Tomorrow is soon enough," Walt said. "Don't try to come back any more today."

"Should we wave a white flag when we come?" I asked.

"Not necessary. And I'm sorry about the gun thing, but you were obviously tailing Dolly, and I didn't know who you were."

"No problem as long as it didn't go off."

We shook hands and I followed in Dolly's tracks, pushing my bike all the way to the blacktop road before mounting it with extreme caution and reluctance. The return trip to Oak Bluffs took a couple of hours longer without Daffy Dolly setting the pace. My leisurely pedaling was interrupted by a rest stop near those bothersome red-white-and-blue beach cabanas, a time out for lunch near the harbor in Edgartown and several stops on the bike path to look at the water and cool my buns.

It was late afternoon when I reached Walt's cottage. The only occupant was Sherlock Holmes, whose greeting reminded me that I had returned without the cat food I'd set out to buy almost seven hours earlier. This time I walked to the store.

When I returned, my four two-legged companions were occupying wicker chairs on the front porch. They had brought out some crackers and cheese, which I could share, and some beer, which, as a recovering alcoholic, I could not.

"Where the hell did you go for that cat food, back to St. Paul?" Al asked.

"You'll have a hard time believing where this cat food hunter has been," I said.

"Okay, hunter, give it a shot," Al replied.

"Yeah, give us both barrels," Dave said.

"Wait a second and I'll get you a root beer," Carol said. That was the best offer I'd had all day.

CHAPTER 6

I'LL NEVER TELL

Just as I expected, Dave Jerome was hot to jump into the borrowed car and drive to Chappy immediately. I eventually convinced him that Walt didn't want to see any more visitors that day and the conversation turned to the dead treasure hunter.

"There are reporters on the island from both Boston papers, the *Providence Journal* and a couple of smaller dailies," Al said. "Also there are a couple of TV crews parked in the lot by the harbor. It's starting to look like our last visit here when we found the missing guy's body after that hellacious windstorm."

"Poor Manny Gouveia," I said. "He's going to have to deal with all those people and cameras again."

"At least he can't blame it on us this time," Al said.

"I don't suppose you're going to join the pack when they call a press conference to announce the autopsy results," Dave said.

"It's tempting," I said. "My bigger problem right now is what to do about your uncle. I don't want to report locating our missing former editor, but Don O'Rourke will kill me if he ever finds out I knew where Walt was hiding and didn't write about it."

"You set yourself up for a lot of work by calling the desk in the first place," Al said.

"How did I know the man was hiding from both the killer

and the cops?" I asked. "We'd all have looked like idiots if Walt had been the next murder victim and we hadn't even told Don that he was missing."

"Well, you can't rat on him now," Dave said. "Is Don expecting a follow to yesterday's story?"

"Are you expecting August to follow July? I'll bet there's a message from Don on my cell phone wondering why in hell I haven't called him."

That was, in fact, the exact text of the message I found on my phone. Luckily, Don had gone home by the time I returned the call, so I talked to Fred Donlin, who is the night city editor and a much less volatile man. I told Fred there was nothing new and he replied that Don had left orders for me to send a follow in time for Tuesday morning's first edition. This meant I'd have to visit the police station after supper and get an official comment.

This was, as Al had said, beginning to feel like our previous visit to the Vineyard. I found myself hoping that this time the ending would be much less painful for me.

The senior officer on duty that night was Detective Harry English, who, like Manny Gouveia, remembered me as the guy the minister almost killed. As I feared, English had nothing new to report. He and Manny had talked to several people and were hoping to interview some others, but as yet there were no official suspects—not even any persons of interest—and the autopsy report that would confirm the death as a homicide wouldn't be ready until Wednesday at the earliest. Don wasn't going to like my story, but what the hell. I mean, I supposedly was here on vacation. Did I think they were going to pay me overtime? Absolutely, on the same day that seahorses flew and carriage horses journeyed to the bottom of the sea.

★ ★ ★

Walt's friend's car turned out to be a 12-year-old Chevy sedan with even more rust on it than the Landrover I'd seen in the woods. We learned later that such rust buckets are known as "island cars," which means they've been exposed to so much seawater and salt-laden air that they're unfit for duty on the mainland. Islanders run them until some major part, such as a tie rod or the floor under the driver's seat, gives way before consigning them to a scrap hauler for disposal.

We decided not to overwhelm Walt with company, so only Dave and Cindy accompanied me on the Tuesday morning drive to Chappaquiddick. As always, the On Time Ferry was on time, but Dave expressed sticker shock at the price: $12 for car and driver and $4 per passenger. Twenty bucks to get us across.

As we passed the Chappaquiddick Beach Club, Dave pointed at the red-white-and-blue cabanas and said, "Look. There's the beach houses that were in 'Jaws.'" Another riddle solved.

I spotted the dirt road that led to Walt's hideout without a problem. We parked and followed the walking path to the campsite, which we found unoccupied. Dave and Cindy were inspecting the Landrover and I was unfolding a lawn chair we'd brought from the cottage when Walt appeared. Again, he was wearing only the cut-off blue jeans and carrying the shotgun.

"By God, it *is* you," Walt said when Dave turned to face him. Walt leaned the gun against a tree and initiated a three-way hug with Dave and Cindy.

"We brought you a replacement for the chair I destroyed," I said when the greetings were finished. Walt laughed and said he'd dumped the broken one into the back of a fisherman's pickup after flattening the truck's tires last night.

"I hope you wiped it clean of fingerprints," I said.

"I wiped off everything except your prints on the arms where you were hanging on during the crash," he said.

After some family small talk, Dave got down to the serious business of trying to persuade Walt to return to Oak Bluffs and talk to the police. Walt gave him the same evasive comments about "circumstances" that he'd given me and said it wasn't safe for him to go home.

"In fact, it would better if you didn't come out here again," Walt said. "If the guy who killed Wade Waters is watching the cottage, he might decide to follow you."

"Why would the killer be watching your cottage?" Dave asked.

"Like I told your reporter friend here, the killer might think I can ID him," Walt replied. "The killer might also think that I've got something he wants."

"What would that be?" I asked.

"The less you know, the better," Walt said. "That way, neither the cops nor the killer can get any info from you."

"You think the killer is going to be asking us questions?" Cindy asked. She'd been wandering around Walt's little camp, examining his living area, but she spun around to face him as she spoke.

"He might," Walt said. "If he thinks you've been talking to me."

"Once and for all, do you know who the killer is?" I asked.

"Not for sure," he said. "My money is on that creepy partner, Charles Morgan, but it could be one of the guys from the Bottoms Up or somebody else who's looking for the Daniel French."

"What about Waters's former partner?" I asked. "The guy Morgan replaced?"

"There's another possibility," Walt said. "His name is Buck Studwell. You might ask the cops if he's been seen on the island."

We finally gave up trying to talk Walt into returning home

and chatted about other things, such as what was happening in St. Paul, how were Dave's and Cindy's kids and what was going on with some other family members. When we were about to leave, Walt said he had something for Dave and went to the front of the van. He returned with a slip of paper.

"This is the cell phone number of a guy named…now don't laugh…Harry Dick," Walt said. "He's an agent and an editor at a syndicate and he wants to talk to you about syndicating your cartoons. He's been summering on the island for years, and I ran into him just before I had to bail out of Oak Bluffs so I didn't get a chance to e-mail you. Anyhow, give him a call when you get back to the cottage."

"Did his parents really name him Harry?" Dave asked.

"Actually, his name is Howard but he calls himself Harry," Walt said. "When you meet him, you'll understand."

"Obviously he's not sensitive about his name," I said.

"Sensitive is not in Harry's vocabulary," Walt said.

"Harry Dick," Dave said. "Sounds like a standup guy."

"Stop it right now," Cindy said before I could get in a line about Dick being a name that wasn't hard to remember.

Dave told Walt that we'd see him again before we left the island and promised that we'd watch for anyone tailing us. After the three Jeromes hugged again, Dave, Cindy and I went back to the car.

"Uncle Walt's always been a little far out, but I think he's gone over the top with all this talk about the killer looking for him," Dave said as I started the engine.

"I just wish he'd put some clothes on," Cindy said. "You'd think the mosquitoes would eat him alive out there in the woods with all that skin exposed."

"Maybe his skin's too tough for the skeeters to penetrate," Dave said.

"Or his blood's too sour for their taste," I said.

"I'm sorry I mentioned it," Cindy said.

When we drove off the On Time ferry into Edgartown, we found traffic even more congested than usual, meaning that even the side streets were gridlocked. We finally worked our way to Main Street where we were confronted by a police officer wearing a glow-orange vest and a passing parade. Flag bearers, bands and make-shift floats flowed past as we waited at the stop sign and a line of cars formed behind us.

"What the hell is going on?" Dave asked. "You'd think it was the Fourth of July."

Cindy looked at her watch, which showed the date as well as the time. "Oh, my god, it *is* the Fourth of July," she said. "I completely lost track of the date."

"Well, happy Independence Day," I said.

"I'd like to be free of this parade," Dave said.

"Be brave and eventually we'll land at home," I said.

After the final marchers passed, the policeman stepped aside and waved us ahead. We fell in behind the tail-enders and crept along behind the parade all the way to the triangle. At that intersection, the marchers moved straight ahead and disbanded while we disembarked to the right and accelerated toward Oak Bluffs. When we arrived, I parked the car alongside Walt's cottage and we were climbing the steps to the porch to join Al and Carol when an Oak Bluffs police cruiser drove up. Detective Manny Gouveia and a uniformed officer emerged.

"What's up, detective?" Dave asked.

"We got here a warrant to search Mr. Walter Jerome's cottage," Manny said, waving a sheet of paper. "We'll try not to mess things up too bad."

"What on earth are you looking for?" Dave asked.

"Maybe you can help us and we won't have to search,"

Manny said. "Have any of you seen a chart of the waters between the Vineyard and Nantucket?"

We all shook our heads.

"Then I guess we'll have to do the search," Manny said. "Is there anybody else inside?"

"Only Sherlock Holmes," I said. "If you don't wake him, he won't be a problem." It's always fun to watch a detective's eyebrows go up, and Manny's were especially black and bushy.

CHAPTER 7

LIFE'S A BEACH

With Dave shadowing Manny Gouveia and Cindy following the uniformed cop, who was introduced as Officer Phillips, the search for the chart commenced. After combing through every room, closet and stairwell, all they'd found was one indignant black cat. Sherlock showed his resentment by hissing at Manny when the detective disturbed him by lifting the mattress to look under it.

"That cat ever do anything but sleep?" Manny asked when he returned to the porch where Al, Carol and I were sitting.

"He's a watch cat," I said.

"Yeah, he watches while you put food in his dish," Al said.

Choosing to ignore this malicious assault on my feline buddy, I tried to question Manny. "What's on this chart and who sent you here to look for it?"

"I ain't authorized to answer no questions," Manny said. "You have to ask either the chief or the DA."

"Will they give us any answers?" I asked.

"I doubt like hell if they'll tell you anything today," he said. "They'll be havin' a press conference tomorrow or the next day when the autopsy on Waters comes in. Maybe you can ask about it then."

That answered Dave's question about whether I'd take time to attend that press conference. The never-to-be-forgotten island vacation he'd promised me was looking even more like my regular forgettable work week in St. Paul.

I couldn't resist asking Manny one more question, even though I knew the answer. "Any word on Walt Jerome?"

"Nothin' yet," the detective said. "But the chief really wants to talk to him about his interview with Waters so he put out an all-island alert."

"Keep us posted on your progress," Al said.

Manny promised that he would, wished us a good day and joined Officer Phillips in the cruiser. After they'd driven away, we three porch sitters went inside to help Dave and Cindy straighten up what the search party had left askew.

We ate a late lunch and decided to drive to State Beach, which was the one that paralleled the bicycle path that we'd followed to Edgartown. We had put in some tanning time previously on the Oak Bluffs public beach, which was only a 10-minute walk from the cottage, but Carol was interested in exploring some new stretches of sand. I voted for change because I was interested in checking out some additional sunbathers of the female variety.

Before we got in the car, Dave put in a call to Harry Dick and left a message on the syndicate editor's voicemail. We'd been lollygagging on the beach for almost two hours, with everyone but me taking an occasional dip in the chilly water, when Dave's cell phone rang.

Dave rose from his beach blanket and walked away to carry on his conversation. When he rejoined us, he said he had a date to meet Harry Dick at 2 p.m. tomorrow at a place called Lucy Vincent Beach.

"Where the hell is that?" Al asked.

"Harry said it's in a town called Chilmark," Dave said. "He gave me directions on how to get there. He said finding the road in is kind of tricky and you need to have some kind of pass to park there, but he's going to meet me in the parking lot."

★ ★ ★

After lunch on Wednesday, Carol and Cindy decided they'd rather take the bus to Edgartown and "do the shops" than ride out to Lucy Vincent Beach, which, according to an island map we found in the cottage, was about 15 miles away.

"Why go all that way to sit on a beach when we've got one within walking distance?" Cindy asked. "To me, a beach is a beach."

"That's a beach of an attitude," Al said.

"She's always beaching about something," Dave said.

"If you add all the beaches together, you get a sum of a beach," I said.

"It's past time for you guys to wave goodbye and go," Carol said.

We departed, with Dave driving, me navigating from the right front seat and Al bringing up the rear. Using the map and following the directions from Harry Dick, we found our way to West Tisbury and a store called Alley's. According to Harry's directions, the road into Lucy Vincent Beach was four and a half miles from that store. It would on our left—a Y-shaped, blacktop road with a light pole in the middle.

Amazingly enough, we spotted the road on our first pass. Dave turned in and within a few feet, the blacktop ended and we bounced along a bumpy, sandy road for almost another half mile before coming to a weathered, barn-shaped building with a sign that said "CHILMARK RESIDENTS ONLY." The sign warned us that parking in the lot beyond this building was for vehicles with beach permits only, and listed a variety of no-no's that included dogs, horses, buses and campfires.

Under the sign was a middle-aged man who stood only about five-foot-six, with black, curly hair, a deep suntan and a belly like Santa Claus. On his face, he wore reflective sunglasses and below his paunch, he wore a black Speedo bikini that was almost lost beneath the flab.

"I feel overdressed," said Dave, who, like Al and I, was wearing conventional swim trunks. "This guy looks like he's barely strapped in." If only he'd known what was coming next.

Dave stopped beside the man, rolled down the window and introduced himself. The man replied, in a louder-than-necessary voice, that he was Harry Dick and he was glad to see us. He slid into the back seat beside Al and told Dave to drive on in. When we encountered the official permit sticker inspector, Harry got out and said a few words to him. I saw Harry slip the man a $20 bill, but I didn't see where he'd been carrying it. I didn't really want to know.

Dave parked the car and we all got out and shook hands with Harry. He led us along a sandy path bordered by a weather-beaten snow fence on the left side and two strands of rope strung between a line of posts on the right. After about 100 yards, the path opened onto a wide expanse of beach. To our right were numerous large, vertical rocks; off in the distance to our left was a high, multi-colored cliff. As always, Al was carrying his camera and he immediately started clicking off some scenic shots.

The sand was much firmer under foot here than it was at the Oak Bluffs and Edgartown beaches, the waves were higher and the air was cooler. There were only half a dozen people in sight, all of them sitting or reclining on blankets. No one was in the water.

"We're camped up this way," Harry said, pointing to the right.

Again, he spoke loud enough to be heard well beyond our group, which seemed to be his style. "I'm here with a lady TV star," he said. "You guys will get a kick out of meeting her."

That proved to be an understatement. As we approached Harry's so-called camp at the base of a 10-foot-tall rock, a young woman with a shape befitting a TV star rose from a beach blanket and came to meet us. Since I was first in line behind Harry, I was the first to shake the hand that the woman offered in greeting. As our hands met, I observed that she was wearing a diamond stud in her navel. I was especially conscious of this bellybutton bauble because it was her sole item of apparel.

"This beautiful lady is Rhonda Fairchild," Harry said as I struggled to shift my eyes upward past two globular, smoothly-tanned breasts to the level of the woman's face. "I'm sure you've seen her on TV in 'Molly Loves Marcia.'"

I had seen Rhonda Fairchild in that sappy sit-com, which was about two lesbians in love, for all of five minutes one night. Blond Rhonda had a round, pretty Scandinavian face and her dark-haired co-star was attractive, too, but five minutes was all I could stomach of the show's stilted dialogue and obtrusive laugh track.

"I thought your face was familiar," I said to Rhonda as I tried to remember which one she played, Molly or Marcia.

"You've hardly looked at my face," Rhonda said. "Why don't you give me an even break and take off your suit?"

"I'm really not into being out of my clothes."

"Harry's got his off. That's what Lucy Vincent Beach is all about." Sure enough, Harry had peeled off the nearly invisible strip of cloth and tossed it onto his blanket.

"Nobody told me this was a nude beach," I said.

"Technically, it's clothing-optional," Rhonda said. "But why would you option to wear a suit when you don't have to?"

"It might be something called embarrassment."

"Oh, pooh! Your friend's got his off, and he looks like a real swinger."

To my chagrin, Dave had stepped out of his swim trunks, putting everything he had on display.

"Yeah, but Dave's a cartoonist," I said. "Cartoonists are natural show-offs."

"What the hell, Mitch," Dave said. "Might as well take it off. Yesterday on the phone, Harry said this is where a lot of celebrities hang out, but I didn't know he meant literally."

My face, which had been cooled by the ocean breeze, grew several degrees warmer with a self-conscious rush of blood as I slid my suit down my legs and pulled it off one foot at a time. Al, the chicken, had spun around and was walking briskly away with his suit in place and his camera hanging from his neck.

"Okay!" Rhonda said with a wide smile as she looked me over. "Everything's in perfect proportion." I took this to mean that she wasn't disappointed by the size of what I'd unveiled.

"Spoken like an expert," I said, trying to be both nonchalant and witty.

"Actually, I am kind of an expert," Rhonda said. "I play a lesbian on TV, but I'm not really a lesbian, you know, and I've spent a lot of time looking at naked men on this beach. Every one I see is different—different sizes, different shapes, even different angles that they hang at. I'm thinking of writing a book about the differences."

"Should be a best seller," I said. "You can call it 'Rhonda Does Know Dick.'"

She giggled. "I might even illustrate it. I'm a pretty good artist, you know. You'd be a good candidate for the cover."

"A seminal work, I'm sure," I replied. Turning to Dave I said, "Tell me again why we're here."

"We're here so I can talk to Harry about syndicating my cartoons," said Dave. "And you can entertain Rhonda while we talk business." Harry had flopped onto a blanket beside Rhonda's and was motioning for Dave to join him.

"I hope Dave's photo on the syndicate's promo blurb won't be full length," I said. Rhonda giggled again and turned toward the blankets, putting some extra swing into her suntanned buns as she walked.

Dave fell in behind Rhonda's seductive behind, and I brought up the rear, feeling grateful that Cindy and Carol hadn't come with us. The thought of being naked in front of my friends' wives—and maybe having them standing naked beside me—sent a shiver through my body.

"So, welcome again to Lucy Vincent Beach," said Harry. "Have a seat, but remember that you gotta be careful, guys. This is where all the pricks hang out." The way he laughed at his own trite witticism reminded me of the sound made by a donkey my dad owned when I was a child.

"And all the titties, too," Rhonda said. "But Mitch has been keeping a close watch on these." She jiggled them for emphasis and giggled for the third time.

Actually, the perky tilt of Rhonda's unsupported breasts made me wonder if they'd been plastically enhanced. Not knowing how to resolve this question, I shifted my attention to the juncture of her lower belly and thighs. Even this décor had been customized. Rhonda had trimmed and shaped her pubic patch like the women who pose for *Playboy* centerfolds. The slender sliver of hair that remained looked like a dark, sharp-tipped spear pointing downward to the pathway to paradise.

Dave and Harry had settled down on the adjacent blanket and were engaged in serious negotiations. I could feel a pulse beating in my groin and decided the only way to avoid an embarrassing incident was to make small talk with Rhonda.

"When did you take up this fascinating study of comparative male anatomy?" I asked.

"Just last week," she said. "The first time Harry brought me out to this beach and we took our suits off. As you must have noticed, Harry doesn't have much to look at below his blubber belly, so I started watching whatever scenery was going by. It's actually a lot of fun, especially for an innocent little girl from Minnesota who never saw a man's cock until she went to New York."

"You're from Minnesota?"

"Yah, sure, you bet'cha. My real name is Mary Margaret Gustafson and I was raised in a little town called Lindstrom where kids only screw in the dark."

"And you were a virgin when you went to New York?"

"I didn't say that. I said I'd never seen a guy's cock."

"So you weren't kidding about only having sex in the dark."

"Norwegians are very private people. It was okay to play with everything as long as you couldn't see it."

"So, how'd you go from Mary Margaret Gustafson to Rhonda Fairchild?" I asked.

"When my agent told me I needed a more theatrical sounding name in order to get work, I thought of the big smiley gopher that walks around the state fair," she said.

"That's right. He's called Fairchild."

"My agent thinks Fairchild's a great last name, and he suggested Rhonda because it's a lot sexier than plain old Mary."

"Let me get this straight," I said. "Now that your name is Rhonda Fairchild instead of Mary Gustafson, it's okay for you to look at men's, um, appendages, as well as touch?"

"Actually I'm pretty much just looking now," Rhonda said. "I don't want my mother to click on an Internet website and see pictures of me getting it on with some guy."

"Good thinking. You can't be too careful these days."

"You got that right." Suddenly, her blue eyes shifted away from mine and I followed her gaze. A young man to whom nature had been more than generous was walking past. "There's one for my book," Rhonda said. "I wish I dared ask him for his measurement."

"Go ahead," I said. "I'm sure he'd be flattered. He might even let you hold the yardstick."

Again she gave me the giggle. "We'd have to do it in the dark."

"Still got that Lindstrom hang-up? What does Harry think about that?"

"Oh, God, I'd never touch Harry. He's a one-man gay pride parade."

That caught me way off guard. "If Harry is gay, why are you staying on the Vineyard with him?"

"He's a real good buddy of my agent and he likes to have what he calls arm candy with him when he travels."

"And this is okay with you?" I asked.

"Why not?" Rhonda said. "I get all the benefits of a free vacation and I don't have to put out for the guy."

Here was a pragmatic woman. I was about to compliment her when Harry and Dave rose to their feet beside us and shook hands. "You got yourself a deal, baby," Harry said in a voice loud enough to be heard by a couple sitting 20 yards away.

Dave thanked him, turned to me and suggested we go find Al. I agreed and we stepped into our swimsuits with such synchronicity that Rhonda said we could be a Broadway dance team.

"Not if we have to do a full Monty onstage," I said.

While Dave and I were saying goodbye to Harry, Rhonda was reaching into her beach bag. She pulled out a brochure for a bed-and-breakfast hotel and handed it to me. "This is where we're staying," she said. "Come and see me after dark." The look in her eyes told me that the innuendo was intentional.

"You sure that's the best time to visit?" I asked.

"Oh, yeah," Rhonda said. She pulled my face down to hers and her bare nipples pressed against my chest as she kissed me lightly on the lips. "Remember, I'm still the shy little girl from Lindstrom."

"Looks like you made a hit with the TV star," Dave said as we walked toward the car.

"I guess I'm okay in her book," I said, and described the book she was planning.

"I bet she won't put Harry in it," Dave said. "For a guy who hasn't got much, he sure talks about it a lot."

"He talked about his dick while you two were dickering?"

"Almost every sentence had a double meaning. Now I know what Uncle Walt meant when he said I'd understand why a guy with the last name of Dick calls himself Harry instead of Howard."

We found Al in the parking lot, sitting on the sand beside the car. "Ah, the exhibitionists return," he said.

"When in Rome, do as Romans do," I said. "You missed a chance to be in a unique publication authored by Rhonda Fairchild."

"I missed a chance to make a damn fool of myself parading around bare-ass on a public beach," he said. "Wait'll the wives hear my beach report."

"I'll beach your head in if you tell Cindy I was out there naked," Dave said. We eventually persuaded Al to promise that our foursome's lack of swimsuits would forever be our little secret.

We arrived home before the women and Dave unlocked the front door. He stepped through into the living room and we heard him yell, "Holy shit!"

Al and I collided and almost got stuck as we leaped through

the door. We stumbled into a room that was in shambles, with chair and sofa cushions scattered all around the floor, the area rug in a heap, two end tables lying on their sides, lamps tipped over and the coffee table upside down.

"The guy might still be in here," I said to Dave. "Call 911." Dave already had his cell phone in his hand as we retreated to the porch.

CHAPTER 8

WHAT'S MISSING?

Two police cruisers appeared in less than three minutes and the uniformed drivers emerged with service weapons drawn. One officer raced around the cottage and went in the back door while the other entered the living room after ordering us to stay on the porch. We could hear them yelling "clear" as they moved from room to room.

"You got a hell of a mess in there but whoever made it is long gone," said the officer who'd started at the front. "You need to take an inventory and see what's missing. They didn't take the TV or the computer or any of the kind of stuff they usually grab."

Wondering about my laptop, I rushed up the stairs to my bedroom and found furniture, blankets, sheets, dresser drawers, all my clothes and the mattress strewn across the floor. One corner of my laptop was peeking out from under a pillow at the foot of the bed. I picked up the computer, put it on the dresser and went back downstairs.

Detective Manny Gouveia had joined Dave and the two uniformed officers in the living room.

"Nothing seems to have been stolen from my room," I said. Dave said their room was a mess but that nothing obvious was missing and Al offered a similar assessment when he appeared.

"Could be your visitor was lookin' for the same thing I was but he wasn't as neat about it," Manny said.

"What the hell is so important about this chart anyway?" Dave asked. "And don't give me that crap about you can't answer any questions."

"I ain't supposed to," Manny said. "But I will tell you that it's connected to Wade Waters and the sunken treasure ship."

"Why would it be here, for God's sake?" Dave asked.

"It's possible that Waters gave it to your uncle," Manny replied.

"Why the hell would he do that?" I asked.

"Your guess is as good as mine," the detective said. "But the person who suggested that we do a search thinks it's possible, and it looks like somebody else does, too. They might even have—"

A woman's scream, pitched slightly above high C, cut him off and we all spun toward the door. The scream had come from Cindy Jerome, who was standing in the doorway with her palms pressed against her cheeks, her eyes stretched as wide as saucers and her mouth hanging open. Carol, looking equally shocked, was a step behind her. Dave leaped toward Cindy and wrapped his arms around her.

"It's okay, Hon," Dave said. "Somebody made a hell of a mess but it looks like they didn't take anything. At least nothing of ours."

"Who would do this?" Cindy asked, looking over Dave's shoulder at Manny.

"We don't know, ma'am," Manny said. "I could call our fingerprint man to come over and see if he can pick up anything, but I'm bettin' that the guy wore gloves. And we'd have to take prints from all five of you for comparison to what he found."

"Forget it," Dave said. "Dusting for prints would just add to the mess and printing all of us would screw up our day even more than it already is."

"How'd anybody get in?" Cindy asked. "I'm sure I locked both doors when Carol and I left the cottage."

"He smashed a pane of glass in the back door," said the officer who'd gone in that way. "Then he reached in and flipped the lock."

As he was leaving, Manny asked us to report any missing items after we'd picked everything up. "I'll talk to the person who requested our search and see if he has any ideas on who else might be lookin' for the chart."

"How about it being the same guy who tossed Waters into the ocean?" I asked.

"That'd be my bet," Manny said. "That's why I'm here checkin' it out. Well, have a good…oh, hell, you ain't gonna have a good night no matter what I say." He walked away shaking his head.

The five of us stood in a circle, surveying the scene in the living room. "Where's that daffy housekeeper now that we need her," Al said.

"Not daffy enough to clean up this mess," Dave said.

"We need to talk to your uncle," I said to Dave as I put the cushions back on the sofa. "He must know what that chart is all about and he might even know where the damn thing is."

"Tomorrow, we visit Uncle Walt, whether he wants the pleasure of our company or not," Dave said.

We worked for an hour straightening the living room, dining room and kitchen. When all our backs were sore, Dave duct-taped a piece of plywood over the broken window and we adjourned to Linda Jean's for supper. After that, we spent a couple more hours restoring order in the various rooms, checking for missing items as we worked. Yes, indeed, I thought as I dragged the mattress back onto my bed, this really is a vacation I'll never forget.

It wasn't until all the furniture, clothing and decorations were back in place in my bedroom that I realized something very important was missing.

"Hey!" I yelled from the hall. "Has anybody seen Sherlock Holmes?"

There was a long silence, followed by a four-voice chorus of "no."

We launched a five-person search of every closet, corner and cranny in the cottage. We looked under every bed, couch, sofa, table and chair. We walked around outside, looking under the bushes with flashlights and calling Sherlock's name. The results were negative.

We gathered in the living room and sat for a moment in gloomy silence.

"The robber or vandal or whatever he was must have left the door open and Sherlock wandered out to explore the world," Carol said. "Don't worry, Mitch, he'll find his way back."

"Put out a dish of food and he'll be back before sunrise," Al said.

"I don't know," I said. "He's not an outdoor cat. It's been years since the last time he had to use his navigation skills."

It was almost 11 p.m., and we were all exhausted from our efforts to create order out of chaos throughout the house, but we decided to stay up long enough to watch the news, which comes on an hour later in the East than it does in the Midwest. After we'd heard all about that day's Boston area shootings, muggings, fires and truck crashes, we caught an item of interest to us. It was a clip of the Dukes County district attorney announcing that he would discuss the results of the Wade Waters autopsy at a press conference at 1 p.m. tomorrow at the Oak Bluffs police station.

Dave turned off the TV after the sports report, and we were all on the way to bed when the phone in the kitchen rang. Dave answered it, said a few words and summoned me. "It's about Sherlock," he whispered as he handed me the phone.

I said hello and a man speaking in a falsetto voice responded. "Are you the guy that owns the big black cat at Walter Jerome's place?" he asked.

"Yes, I am," I said, hoping he was about to bring Sherlock back to me.

Instead, he sent me into a state of panic. "If you want to see your cat alive again, you've got 24 hours to produce the chart," he said.

"What chart are you talking about?" I asked.

"Don't play stupid with me, asshole. I want the chart that Walter Jerome has got."

"Nobody knows where Walter Jerome is."

"Then you'd better fuckin' find him or your kitty cat goes for a swim."

"If you hurt one hair on that cat's head—"

"What'll you do, big man, dive into the ocean after him?" the high-pitched voice asked. "Now you listen and listen close. I'm gonna call again at this same time tomorrow night. When I do, you'd better have that chart in your hands and be prepared to deliver it to me if you want to see your cat again. And I don't want to see no cops hangin' around when you make the delivery. Have a nice night, pussy lover."

The line went dead and I stood holding the receiver, staring into a semi-circle of four quizzical faces. "Now we *really* need to see your uncle first thing in the morning," I said.

CHAPTER 9

A FOLLOWING

Dave, Al and I drove away from the cottage at 7 a.m. after leaving a message with the police desk sergeant to have Detective Gouveia call my cell phone as soon as he got in. Remembering Walt's warning about being followed, Al and I kept checking the road behind us as we drove along the beach road toward Edgartown.

As we neared the triangle, Al, who was in the back seat, said that a black Altima had been behind us all the way. "It might be a coincidence, but maybe we should pull into that little shopping area at the triangle and let him go on by."

Dave agreed. "There's a doughnut shop in the triangle," he said. "I'll pull in and one of you can run in and get us some coffee."

There were two entrances to the mini-mall from the road we were on. Dave took the first one and the black Altima, which had been lagging quite a distance back, continued on its way. Dave made a loop through the parking lot and stopped in front of the doughnut shop. When we stopped, we saw the Altima parked inside the second entrance. The windows of the Altima were tinted, but we could see the silhouettes of two people seated in the front.

Al went into the shop and returned with three cups of coffee and a bag of doughnuts, two plain-glazed and one (for me) with chocolate frosting.

"Now comes the test," Dave said as he pulled out of the parking lot. A few seconds later, the Altima was behind us again.

"He's not very subtle," Al said.

"A real klutz at tailing people," I said. "But whatever he is, we can't go near the On-Time Ferry until we've lost him."

The problem was that we didn't know how to go about shaking a tail in a town we weren't familiar with. Dave had only a superficial knowledge of Edgartown's streets from previous visits, and Al and I could offer no help.

"Maybe I can trap him in traffic down by the harbor," Dave said. He drove straight down Main Street until it dead-ended in a parking lot between two harbor-side restaurants. Unfortunately, we were too early for the heavy tourist traffic that usually chokes Edgartown in July, so the Altima was still in sight when we exited the parking lot and started up a hill on a one-way street.

That street T'd into another one-way street, which Dave took to the right. This street grew narrower as it wound past a couple of high-buck hotels and hooked back almost 180 degrees to the left after providing us with a view of the Edgartown lighthouse off to the right. Dave rounded the curve as fast as he dared and for a moment we thought we'd lost the Altima, but it soon reappeared a block behind us.

"I don't know where to go next," Dave said. "We need to fake him out somewhere, but I don't know where."

"What about a couple of miles back out of town, where the road takes a sharp turn by a little parking lot that overlooks the beach?" I said. "We could start back toward Oak Bluffs, flip a quick U-ey in that parking lot and meet our pals in the Altima still going the other way."

"Worth a try," Dave said. "Providing I can find the way back to the road that goes to Oak Bluffs." We were in a residential area, zigzagging our way through a maze of narrow streets to wherever they might lead. Suddenly, miraculously, we were at a stop sign at an intersection with the street we'd taken from the triangle to downtown. The Altima was still a block behind us.

Dave turned right and retraced our route, driving past the triangle and continuing toward Oak Bluffs. As we rounded a curve and neared the beach with the small parking area, Dave suddenly floored the gas pedal and the Altima dropped out of sight. It was still out of sight when Dave zipped through the parking lot, drawing an impromptu epithet and a middle-finger salute from a pot-bellied man in a paisley swimsuit, spun the Chevy around and headed back toward Edgartown at 50 miles per hour. Seconds later, we met the Altima, and Dave stepped the gas pedal down even harder.

"They'll never catch us if we can get into the Edgartown traffic before they see us again," Dave said. "We'll duck up a side street and wait awhile before we head for the ferry landing."

We were not quite back to the triangle, hitting about 60 miles per hour, when a blue light flashed behind us.

"Oh, shit!" Dave said. "We're going to be pulled over for speeding."

He pulled as far to the right as possible, stopping with two wheels on a very narrow shoulder and the other two still in the traffic lane. An Edgartown police cruiser with its lights flashing drew to a stop behind us. After talking briefly on his radio, the cop got out, walked cautiously up to Dave's window and requested his license and registration. He was just asking about the disparity between Dave's Minnesota driver's license and the car's Massachusetts registration in the name of a different person when the black Altima cruised slowly past us.

I turned around and spoke to Al. "That bastard will be waiting for us at the triangle."

"Did you say something to me, sir?" the cop asked, peering through the window past Dave.

"Nothing at all, officer," I said, hoping he hadn't caught the word "bastard" and thought it applied to him. "Nothing at all." At that moment, my cell phone rang. It was Manny Gouveia returning my call.

The Edgartown cop took the license and registration back to his cruiser to check them out while I was telling Manny about my kidnapped kitty and the late-night phone call demanding the mysterious chart as ransom.

Manny's response was predictable. "Why in the goddamn hell did you bring a cat with you to the Vineyard?"

"Because I didn't want to leave him with somebody else for two weeks," I said. "I did that last fall when I went to Cape Verde to visit my girlfriend."

"How come you've got a girlfriend in Cape Verde?"

"I lead a very complicated life. But right now, my main interest is getting my cat back all in one piece."

"Well, we still ain't found either the chart or Walt Jerome, so there ain't much we can do for you except to keep lookin'," Manny said.

"We're looking, too," I said. "And we're being followed by somebody while we're looking." I told him about the black Altima tailing us all morning.

"Try to get his plate number and we'll check out the owner," Manny said. Al was waving a piece of paper in front of my face and pointing to a number he'd written on it. I recited this number to Manny and he said he'd call back after running it through the registration computer.

"Anything else I can do for you right now?" Manny asked.

The Edgartown cop was handing Dave a ticket and saying he'd clocked us at 58 miles per hour in a 35 zone but was only writing the ticket for 50 because we were visitors to the island.

"Uh, well, if you have any pull with the Edgartown PD you might help us get rid of a speeding ticket," I said.

"The day Edgartown PD tears up a speeding ticket will be the day that hell freezes over," Manny said. "Those guys would ticket the chief's grandmother in her wheel chair if she was goin' over 35."

Before returning to his cruiser, Edgartown's finest delivered a short lecture on the need for driving slowly and carefully on the island. Then he waited behind us until Dave pulled completely into the driving lane.

"We can't go past the triangle," Al said. "If we do, those assholes in the Altima will pick us up."

"What else can we do?" Dave asked. "I don't know any other way to get into Edgartown."

"What about the map we used to find our way to that naked beach?" Al asked. "Why don't we stop somewhere and look it over?"

"There is no place to stop between here and the triangle," Dave said. I suggested turning around in the next driveway and going back to the parking lot by the beach. This required a left turn into a road marked "Cow Bay," which Dave executed slowly and carefully after making sure to signal for the benefit of the police officer still behind us.

Studying the map, we discovered that if we went back to Oak Bluffs, we could pick up County Road, which would take us to Edgartown-Vineyard Haven Road. This was a long, out-of-the-way loop, but it would allow us to pass the triangle on the opposite side, behind the watchers in the Altima. We decided it was worth a try.

It was almost half an hour later when we cruised past the triangle. We didn't see the Altima in the parking lot, but Dave didn't linger to get a closer look.

"They might have got tired of waiting," I said. "They'd have expected to see us right after the cop went by. When we didn't show up, they might have gone home."

"Or moved to a different spot," Dave said.

"There they are," Al said. And there was the Altima, in a restaurant parking lot on our right. Dave couldn't speed up because of the cars ahead of us and we crawled past at about 10 miles per hour. Al and I watched without breathing for what seemed like hours until the motionless Altima was out of sight.

"Guess they went in for coffee," Al said after taking a big gulp of air.

"Probably needed perking up," I said.

"If somebody hired them to tail us, that coffee break is grounds for firing," Al said.

"Well, anyway, their job has gone to pot," I said.

My cell phone rang, interrupting this brilliant exchange of witticisms. It was Manny Gouveia reporting that the Oak Bluffs PD had run the license plate number and learned that the Altima was a rental car. It had been leased in Vineyard Haven the previous day by a Dirk Oberman, who had displayed a Florida driver's license.

"Any idea what he's doing up here?" I asked.

"As a matter of fact, I do," Manny said. "He just happens to be the owner of that treasure hunter boat that's anchored over in Vineyard Haven."

"The Bottoms Up?"

"That's the one."

"I suppose there's nothing you guys can do about them following us."

"Not unless they get too close to your back bumper," Manny said. "Then we can tag'em for tailgatin'."

"Very funny," I said. "Maybe we'll have a little chat with Mr. Oberman later on."

"I wouldn't get too chippy with him if I was you. They ain't the prettiest lookin' crew in the world."

"Thanks," I said. "We'll be careful. Anyway, we seem to have lost them for now." At that moment, I was thinking that the Bottoms Up boys couldn't look any less pretty than Cap'n Charles Morgan, whom we'd met on the All That Glitters.

Walt was as happy to see us as a three-legged mouse that finds itself nose-to-nose with a hungry cat. "I thought I told you to stay the hell away from here," he said as we strolled single-file into his campsite.

"Things in the real world have gotten personal," I said. "You need to take a break from saving those piping whatever-they-ares and help us save my meowing cat."

We recited the tale of the bothersome break-in, the purloined pussycat and the frightening phone call. When we'd finished, Walt sighed and said, "Shit!"

"My sentiment exactly," Al said. "Now tell us what you know about the mysterious chart."

Walt sighed again. "As you've probably figured out, it shows precisely where the wreck of the Daniel French lies."

"You mean Waters found the wreck before he took his final swim?" Dave asked.

"He told me off the record that he did," Walt said. "And he wrote the geographic coordinates on a chart. Only he did it in code."

"Does anybody else know the code?" I asked. "Charles Morgan, for example."

"I'm pretty sure that Waters didn't share it with anyone," he said. "I think Morgan knows the general area, but he doesn't have the coordinates or the code."

"Which means he's looking for the chart and hoping to figure it out," Dave said. "Do you have any idea where the chart is?"

"It's in my glove compartment," Walt said, pointing toward the Landrover.

CHAPTER 10

TRADE BAIT

Walt spread the chart out on the hood of the Landrover. There was no "X-marks-the-spot" like you see on the movie pirate maps; just a series of letters that Walt believed would show the latitude and longitude of the wreck when decoded.

"Why'd he give you this?" Dave asked.

"He said he thought somebody was trying to steal it," Walt said. "He told me to hide it until he asked to have it back. Obviously, he isn't going to ask."

"He didn't give you the code?" I asked.

"No, he didn't," Walt said. "I'm not sure if that would be good or bad if the guy who ransacked my cottage ever got hold of me."

"He'd probably try to beat it out of you," Dave said.

"Which is another good reason for me not to be found," Walt said.

"There are more letters than you'd need for two sets of degrees, minutes and seconds," Al said.

"He probably threw in some extra shit to make the code tougher to break," Walt said. "I've tried to figure it out but I can't get anywhere with it."

"We need to take this back to Oak Bluffs," Dave said. "We have to trade it for Mitch's pussycat."

"Is your cat really that important to you?" Walt asked.

"Damn right he is," I said. "He's been my roommate for almost 10 years. He even saved our lives once when a nut-cake woman was going to shoot five of us."

Walt folded the chart and handed it to me. "Be sure you make a copy before you give it to the sleazebag. And hide it somewhere not in my house."

"We'll bring it back to you," Dave said.

"I'd rather you didn't come back here, but if you insist on doing that, make damn sure nobody follows you," Walt said.

"Maybe we could send it out with Daffy Dolly," I said.

"Stay the hell away from Dolly," Walt said. "If you're being watched and those bastards see you contacting her, they'll latch onto her and God knows what they'll do to that poor woman."

We agreed to keep our distance from Dolly and to handle the copy of the chart with the utmost caution. Then we said goodbye to Walt and returned to our car. It was almost noon and I had a 1 p.m. news conference to attend in Oak Bluffs.

We watched for the Altima all the way back to the cottage, but it was nowhere in sight.

★ ★ ★

Most of the members of the media pack had left the island earlier in the week, but the troops were back in full force to hear the autopsy report. Dave and Al tagged along with me as I joined the gaggle of reporters, photographers and TV cameramen elbowing for position in front of the Oak Bluffs police station.

At precisely 1 p.m., Oak Bluffs Police Chief Darryl Forbush and Dukes County Attorney Elizabeth Winthrop stepped out to face us.

Forbush was a tall, angular man in his 50s who looked fit enough to run a marathon. Winthrop was a sturdy, dark-haired woman of about 40 with piercing brown eyes, broad hips and wide shoulders. Neither Forbush in his uniform nor Winthrop in her dark blue pantsuit was dressed appropriately for a humid, 88-degree afternoon in July. Consequently, the sweat quickly began to bead up on their faces as they surveyed the T-shirt-and-shorts-clad mob in front of them.

Winthrop took the lead, telling us that Wade Waters had a severe contusion on the back of his head and that no water had been found in his lungs. "The medical examiner has determined that Mr. Waters was dead when he went into the ocean and that a blow to the head with a blunt instrument was the cause of death," she said. "The ME also found a number of contusions on the victim's face, arms and torso that indicated a possible struggle with his assailant."

Or a beating and torture, I said to myself. Each blow could have been an attempt to persuade the victim to reveal the location of the chart.

The county attorney went on with the usual crap about an investigation being under way and her office having full confidence that the killer would be identified and brought to justice. When she paused to catch her breath, the volley of questions began. Had anyone been questioned? Were there any suspects? What was the killer's motive? Had Waters located the wreck with the gold?

Winthrop dodged them all by saying it was too early to speculate on suspects, motivation or the location of the sunken ship. If she was aware of the existence of the coded chart, she kept her knowledge to herself. Forbush, who obviously knew about the chart, said nothing before leading Winthrop back into the serenity of the police station.

"No surprises there," Al said as we walked back to join the women for a late lunch on the porch. "And as for the motive, well, duh—the dead guy was hunting for sunken treasure."

"TV reporters need to ask dumb questions like that because they're on camera and they have to look like they're actually doing something," I said. "What seems strange to me is that I just went to a news conference and I don't have to write about it."

"Yeah, and I didn't have to shoot any pix," Al said.

"I thought I saw you shooting," I said.

"Well, I did shoot a few of the chief and the DA and the crowd just out of habit. It's like we're halfway working and halfway on vacation."

"Didn't I promise you guys a vacation you'd never forget?" Dave asked.

"Remind me to have an appointment for something more pleasant, like a root canal, the next time you invite me to the Vineyard," I said.

Before Dave could reply, my cell phone rang and I was greeted by City Editor Don O'Rourke. "What's going on with our missing former editor?" he asked. "We're getting phone calls from people who remember him."

"Walt is still officially missing," I said. "And we just heard that the last guy he interviewed was killed by a blow to the head after having the crap beat out of him." This much was true.

"Do they think Walt did it?" Don asked.

"No way. But the cops do want to talk to him about the case, so they may locate him eventually."

"We need an update for tomorrow. Send a few 'graphs to the night city editor for the early morning run."

"Do I get comp time for all the work I've been doing on my vacation?"

"Just take your laptop to the beach with you and knock something out between gawking at the babes in bikinis."

I wanted to tell him that the only bikinis I'd seen to date were worn by two unattractive men, but I decided to be discreet. "Using my laptop on a sandy beach should add some true grit to my story," I said.

"God, how I miss your down-to-earth humor," Don said as he hung up. I felt that his tone indicated a lack of sincerity.

★ ★ ★

After lunch, we turned on Walt's computer and put the chart into his copier.

"Should we make more than one copy?" Dave asked.

"Every copy we have increases the chance of having one stolen," Cindy said. "I wish you wouldn't even make one."

"Uncle Walt's orders," he said. "But you're right. I will stop with one."

Our next problem was where to put our copy until we could sneak it out to Walt's Chappaquiddick camp. After a 10-minute debate, we decided to put the chart into a second-hand envelope that had formerly contained Walt's electric bill and lay it at the bottom of the plastic grocery bag lining the bathroom wastebasket. Carol tucked it under a disgusting pile of used Kleenexes, empty toilet paper rolls, crushed paper drinking cups and stained Q-tips.

"Perfect," she said. "No man would ever lower himself to look in a wastebasket."

"Hey!" Al said. "I looked in a wastebasket once."

"Only because you knocked your toothbrush into it," Carol said.

Now all we had to do was kill nine hours while waiting for the catnapper's 11:30 call. The consensus was to spend the first two hours on the beach—the one within walking distance. After that, we could watch the world go by from our porch while adjusting our attitudes with food and drinks.

I lagged behind on the beach excursion because I felt a desperate need to talk to Martha Todd. It was 6:30 p.m. in Cape Verde, which meant she should be in her apartment having dinner. I found a spot in Ocean Park where my cell phone had its strongest signal and punched in Martha's number. All I got was her answering machine asking me to leave a message.

"Please call me as soon as you're in," I said. "I really, really need you." Then I pocketed the phone and went to find the rest of the crew.

We'd finished our sun-tanning stint on the beach, everyone had showered and we were parked on the porch with nibbles and drinks when my phone finally rang. "Hi," Martha said. "Sorry I missed your call, but some of us went out for dinner."

"Anyone I know?" I asked. I had met several of her fellow lawyers during my winter visit to Cape Verde.

"Amy and John," she said. "You know them. And Frederico."

Frederico was a name I knew and a name I hadn't wanted to hear. He was 26 years old and recently divorced, and if the term "stud-muffin" had been illustrated in Webster's dictionary his picture would have appeared. Frederico was tall and muscular, with light brown-skin that matched Martha's, and he had a dazzling smile like the come-hither guys on TV commercials who invite you to vacation on their island.

Martha kept telling me that Frederico wasn't interested "that way" in an older (39) woman like her, but I knew better. Frederico was male and had eyes, which meant he was interested "that way" in Martha, who had the body of a 25-year-old sexpot movie star and a smile that out-dazzled his. I could only hope that Martha would never become interested "that way" in Frederico.

"Your message sounded like the sky was falling," Martha said. "What's wrong on the beautiful Vineyard?"

"Sherlock Holmes has been stolen," I said.

"You let somebody take Sherlock?" I swear she'd have sounded more sympathetic if I'd said I'd shot my grandmother.

"I didn't *let* anybody take him. There was nobody home and some asshole broke in, trashed the house and took off with Sherlock. Then he called and demanded ransom."

"You're paying it, aren't you?"

I said that I was and told her the entire story. By the end of my tale, Martha was in a more forgiving mood and she instructed me to call her the instant that Sherlock Holmes was safe in my arms. We had exchanged some kissy sounds and were saying goodnight for the third time when the battery in my cell phone crapped out.

"What's Martha been doing?" Al asked.

"Having dinner with Frederico," I said.

"The divorced stud who's supposedly not interested in Martha's aging body?"

"That's the one."

"You're lucky she's bringing her body home in three months," Al said. Martha's three-year commitment to serve the public in the Cape Verde attorney general's office would expire on October 31, which meant she should be back in St. Paul by November 1.

"I hope she's bringing it home in three months," I said. "You never know what she might get talked into."

"Like sharing it with Frederico?"

"Don't even mention the possibility."

"You might have to go over there and drag her to the airplane by the hair, caveman style."

"Her ex-husband dragged her around the kitchen floor by the hair, caveman style, which is the reason he's an ex," I said.

"Well, let's hope she doesn't cave in to Frederico's charms," Al said.

"That would certainly leave me in the hole."

★ ★ ★

At 11:25 that night, I was standing beside the kitchen phone with my hand hovering above it, ready to grab the receiver at the first faint tinkle of the bell.

"Try not to be too eager," Al said, pulling my hand down to my side. "At least let the first ring finish."

"Easy for you to say," I said, yanking my hand away from his. "Who knows if that bastard has been giving Sherlock any food or water?"

The clock moved along to 11:30, 11:31 and 11:32 before the phone rang. By that time, I'd let my hand drop out of exhaustion, but I managed to grab the receiver before it rang a second time.

"Are you the cat owner?" said the same phony falsetto voice.

"I am," I said. "And I want him back immediately."

"Hold your horses, cowboy. First we have to make some arrangements."

"I want to hear from the cat so I know he's okay. Put the phone next to his head."

"No fuckin' way, man. The sumbitch bites."

"Good. I hope those bacteria I painted on his teeth give you a horrible, lingering, flesh-eating disease."

"Oh, cut the bullshit. The only poison he's got in his mouth is a breath that stinks like fish. Now are you ready to deliver the chart?"

I said I was ready to trade the chart for the cat as soon as possible.

"Okay," Falsetto Voice said. "Do you know where the outdoor basketball court with the fancy electric scoreboard is in Oak Bluffs?"

"I have no clue," I said. "I've never seen it."

"It's on the corner of Pocasset and Wamsutta, maybe a five-minute walk from where you are. I want you to come alone with the chart in an envelope, and leave it next to the post holding up the basket closest to Pocasset. Then you turn your ass around and walk straight back to your house without lookin' over your shoulder. I'll be watchin' you, and I'll also be watchin' for cops."

"Will my cat be there when I leave the envelope?"

"Your cat'll be there when I put him there. You just make damn sure the chart is there before my watch says it's midnight."

"What if I can't find the court that soon?" It was already 11:35.

"Then your fat old cat goes for a swim with the sharks," he said. "Anybody with half a fuckin' brain should be able to find that basketball court in less than 25 minutes."

"When will you give me my cat?" I asked. But the line was dead. Falsetto Man had hung up.

"Get the Oak Bluffs map," I yelled as I hung up the phone. "We have to find a street named Pocasset."

"Is that anything like a streetcar named Desire?" Al asked.

"Right now I'm on a trolley named Desperate and I have to track down a basketball court before the clock strikes twelve," I said.

"Here's the map," Dave said.

"Okay," I said. "It's Pocasset or bust for my pussycat."

"Let's hope it's the catnapper who gets busted," Al said.

"There's no way we can get him busted," I said. "If we tell the cops that we've got the chart, they'll know that we found Walt and we'll have to tell them where he is."

"We can't give them Uncle Walt until he says he's ready," Dave said. "It would have been better if you hadn't told that detective about Sherlock being stolen. Now he's going to be following up and asking questions about how you got Sherlock back."

"We could tell Gouveia that we phonied-up a chart and gave it to the scumbag," I said.

"Lots of luck lying to a cop," Dave said. "I'll bet that's against the law even in Oak Bluffs."

"Let's worry about that tomorrow," I said. "My immediate problem is finding that basketball court."

We located the designated intersection on the map. Falsetto Voice was right—the court was only a short walk from the cottage. With the Oak Bluffs map and a flashlight in one hand and the coded chart in the other, I set off in what I hoped was the right direction at 11:42. The street was as dark as the inside of a whale's belly. There were no streetlights, and the clouds that had begun drifting in from the west shortly before sunset were blanketing the entire sky and blotting out the moon, which had been bright and gibbous the previous night.

Crossing what I believed to be the last street before Pocasset, I turned on the flashlight and searched for a sign. I had learned that, unlike Minnesota, street signs here were at a minimum, the New England attitude being that if you didn't know where you were, you didn't belong there. True to form, there was no sign at this corner, but I continued onward in blind faith.

I'd gone another half a block when I heard a footstep behind me. I started to turn around and got only far enough to see something coming toward my head. The next thing I saw was the beam of the flashlight and Al's face inches from mine.

Gradually, I became aware that I was lying on the ground and my head felt like someone was pounding on it with a hammer. I groaned.

"About time you woke up," Al said, backing off a couple of feet. "You've been napping so long that I started hunting for a pulse."

"Have I got one?" I asked. I started to sit up but a shot of additional pain convinced me to lay my head down again. "Where the hell am I?"

"You're half a block from the basketball court. I was tailing along about a block behind you so I didn't get a look at the guy who whacked you and grabbed the chart."

"Where's Sherlock? Did he leave Sherlock?"

"Not here. Maybe he's at the basketball court."

Again, I tried to sit up. This time I made it, but Al put his hands on my shoulders and prevented me from trying to stand. "Sit there a minute," he said. "I'll go check the court." He disappeared into the darkness.

I put my hand up behind my right ear to caress the central source of my cranial discomfort and found a lump that felt as big as a basketball. In the distance, I heard men's voices shouting, one of which I identified as Al's.

Now what the hell, I wondered. A couple of minutes later, this question was answered as Al returned with a two-man escort. He had nothing in his hands except the flashlight.

"Sorry," he said. "Looks like the bastard still has your cat."

"You sure as hell know how to find trouble," Detective Manny Gouveia said as he knelt beside me.

"What are you doing here?" I asked.

"We almost arrested your buddy when he started prowlin' around the basketball court," the detective said. "We was waitin' for the cat stealer to pick up his package but obviously he decided to grab it before you got to the drop point."

"How did you—"

He cut me off in mid-question. "We got a warrant and put a tap on your phone while you was gone this afternoon. I listened in on your little chat with the cat grabber, and me and Sergeant Donatelli staked out the court."

"You tapped our phone without telling us?" I said.

"We'd have gotten around to that eventually," he said. "We was more concerned with nailin' this guy when you gave him the chart."

"Apparently, he decided not to wait until I put the envelope under the basket," I said.

"Probably he was plannin' to whack you here right from the start and followed you all the way from the cottage," Manny said. "How's the head?" He turned on his flashlight and aimed it at the lump.

"I think I need some ice," I said.

"You sure as hell need somethin'," he said. "That lump is as big as a goddamn egg."

"Is that all?" I said. "I was thinking along the lines of a balloon—the kind you ride in."

"You might want to check in at the emergency room to see if you've got a concussion," Manny said. "I can take you to the hospital."

I started to shake my head but quickly stopped the motion. "That's okay," I said. "I'll just put some ice on it at the cottage."

"Whatever you say," he said. "Sit tight for a minute while I get my truck and I'll run you back home. I've got some questions for you guys anyhow."

Manny drove Al and me to the cottage in an aged Chevy pickup that had enough rust to qualify as an island car and accompanied us into the living room. While Cindy and Carol clucked over me like mother hens and applied a dishtowel packed with smashed ice cubes to my lump, Manny quizzed Dave and Al about the whereabouts of Walt Jerome. After some hemming and hawing, the detective threatened to charge Dave with protecting a fugitive.

"He's not a fugitive," Dave said.

"Tell that to the judge when I take you into court tomorrow

morning after keepin' you in a cell overnight," Manny said. That ended the discussion, with Dave agreeing to lead Manny to Walt's hiding place at 10 the next morning.

Manny departed, I washed down a couple of aspirin, and we all gathered in the living room to talk about the unhappy turn of events. We agreed there was nothing further to be done until morning and were starting to head for our respective bedrooms when the phone rang. Cindy answered, listened for a moment and summoned me.

"Pretty cute," Falsetto Voice said. "Givin' me coordinates in a fucked-up code. Now I want the code."

"I want my cat, you son of a bitch," I said. "You've had a cheap shot at me and you've got your damn chart. Now give me my cat."

"You know damn well that the chart's no good without the code. You give me the code and I'll give you the cat."

"I don't have the code. Nobody does. The code went to heaven along with Wade Waters."

"I don't believe that for a minute," he said. "Walt Jerome has the fuckin' code and I want it by tomorrow night. I'll be callin' at the usual time to set up another meetin'."

"You're wasting your time," I said. "Walt hasn't got the code, so you might as well bring back my cat right now."

"Don't you wish? Listen to what I'm sayin', Mister Pussy Lover. I get the code tomorrow or you don't get the cat until he floats up in the harbor." The line went dead and I shouted out a long string of obscenities without once repeating myself as I put down the phone.

"I'm impressed with your vocabulary," Cindy said when I returned to the living room. I apologized for my language and told them what Falsetto Voice had said.

"You're screwed," Dave said. "I think Uncle Walt was telling the truth when he said Waters didn't give him the code."

"Me, too," I said. "That means we're going to have to fake the code, set up a meeting and trap the bastard so we can rescue Sherlock."

"Let's talk about it in the morning," Al said. "My head's starting to hurt as much as yours."

"Good idea," I said. "We should all be fresh when we plan the next bit of entertainment for this island vacation that we'll never forget."

"I'll sure as hell remember never to promise anybody anything like that again," Dave said.

I rose from my chair and took a step toward the stairs. Suddenly, the room began to whirl like a carousel, and then the lights went out.

The next thing I saw was the living room ceiling and, strangely enough, the ceiling was moving. When I tried to sit up, I discovered it was me and not the ceiling that was moving. I was strapped to a gurney rolling toward the front door.

"Hey," I said. "Where are we going?" My voice sounded far away.

"You're going to the hospital," Carol said. "You passed out and scared us half to death." Her hand was on mine, but her voice also sounded far away.

"But I'm okay now," I said as the gurney passed through the front door.

"Tell it to the folks in the ER," Carol said. "Al will follow you in the car so he can bring you home if they don't keep you overnight."

By the time the two EMTs rolled me into the emergency room, the world was back in focus and all the voices, mine and theirs, sounded normal. I told them I was feeling much better and should just go home, but they wheeled me into a curtained cubicle, undid my bonds and slid me onto a narrow bed. "Have a good night," they said as they departed. Oh, yeah, it had been great so far.

The night got better a moment later when a slender, dark-haired nurse gently took my hand in hers, smiled down at me and said, "Welcome to ER. My name is Zee. What's yours?"

CHAPTER 11

A SHOT IN THE DARK

Tests showed that I had a mild concussion, so they kept me overnight for observation. This entailed walking with the lovely Zee every hour, which was pleasant but exhausting. After breakfast, I was told to go home and get lots of rest. Al came to get me and I fell asleep while fastening my seatbelt.

Dave had gone to Chappy with Gouveia, so the rest of us gathered on the porch and I managed to stay awake to discuss strategy. We surmised that Falsetto Voice would give me another quick-time, nearby ransom drop point and would intercept me before I got there again. He probably suspected that the cops were tapping the phone line. This meant we had to be ready for his surprise attack so we could launch a counter-offensive, bring him down and rescue Sherlock.

"Too bad I couldn't bring my pepper spray along on the flight to Boston," Cindy said. "You could hit the scumbag with a shot of that."

"You're licensed to carry pepper spray?" I asked.

"I am," she said. "I carry it when I work nights at the library. But I don't know where to get it on the Vineyard."

"We could ask our friendly, neighborhood detective about getting some pepper spray when he comes back," Al said.

"He'll want to know why I want it after being here for almost a week without it," Cindy said. "He'll find out what we're planning and order us not to do the vigilantes bit. We need a weapon that we can buy without having to deal with the cops."

We were still trying to formulate a plan, having rejected the use of a knife as requiring too close contact and a baseball bat as requiring too much accuracy, when the Oak Bluffs PD cruiser returned at about 11:30. I was half expecting to see Walt Jerome sitting in the back seat wearing handcuffs, but the rear compartment was unoccupied. Dave got out and Detective Gouveia drove away.

"So what happened?" the four of us asked in unison.

"Uncle Walt wasn't there," Dave said. "The Landrover was gone and the campsite was cleaned up like nobody had ever been there." All four of us expressed amazement, again in unison.

"No clue as to where he went?" I asked.

"He didn't leave his forwarding address tacked to a tree," Dave said. "Apparently he got tired of entertaining guests."

"This is very disappointing after all you told us about his legendary hospitality," Al said.

"I'll remember not to brag about that anymore, either," Dave said.

"So now we know for sure that we can't get the code to trade for Sherlock Holmes," I said.

"Dead certain," Dave said.

"Don't use that word when we're talking about my cat."

"How many of his nine lives do you think he has left?" Dave asked.

"He's used up a couple living with me," I said. "I don't know how many he went through before that."

"We'd better base our rescue strategy on the assumption that Sherlock only has one life left," Carol said. "Now what are we going to do?"

We decided the planning would go better if we had some nourishment, so Cindy called a Circuit Avenue pizza shop for a couple of take-outs. I stayed on the porch in deference to the drum beats in my head while Dave and Al went off to get the pizzas. When they returned, they put the boxes on the largest wicker table and we all helped ourselves.

"Damn!" I said as my first slice slid off the paper plate and onto my lap. The result was a tomato-sauce stain on a pair of khaki shorts that I'd bought especially to wear on the Vineyard. I went into the kitchen to wash off the red splotch as best I could, and when I returned to the porch, I learned that my accident had steered Dave's mind onto a track that led to a plan for capturing the culprit incarcerating my cat.

We polished off the pizza and put the empty boxes on the kitchen counter prior to piling into the car and driving to Edgartown. In a store Dave had seen there, we procured the weapons necessary for our upcoming confrontation with Falsetto Voice.

While in Edgartown, we debated taking the On Time Ferry over to Chappaquiddick and searching for Walt. We decided such an excursion would be a waste of time, given our meager knowledge of the island's hiding places, so we turned back toward Oak Bluffs.

The battleship-gray clouds that had darkened the Vineyard sky all morning were gone and reflections of the sunlight were dancing on the ripples as we drove along the road paralleling State Beach. The sight was so enticing that we decided to forget our problems for a while by changing into swimsuits at the cottage and returning for a respite at the beach. I had little enthusiasm for this because of the endless, dull ache in my head, but I went along for the ride and actually dozed off on a blanket while the others splashed around in the water.

Back at the cottage, we flopped into chairs on the porch with cold libations in hand—beer for Al, Dave and Cindy, gin and tonic for Carol and ginger ale for Mitch.

"Shower time," Al said after draining the last drops of his beer.

"Right," Cindy said. "First I'm going to get those pizza boxes out of the kitchen before they draw ants or flies or something."

"I thought you'd already taken them out," Carol said. "I was going to toss them after mixing my drink but they were gone."

We all looked at each other.

"I didn't throw them out," Dave said.

"It wasn't me," Al said.

"Oh, shit!" I said and ran to the first-floor bathroom. There I looked for the wastebasket into which we'd buried our copy of the treasure map under 12 inches of trash. Now the basket contained only a fresh, empty plastic grocery bag liner.

I raised the wastebasket and tilted it toward four pairs of eyes staring in through the bathroom door. "Daffy Dolly," I said. "Friday must be cleaning day."

We all dashed to the backdoor like a stampede of buffalo. Al reached the big gray trash barrel first and yanked off the cover. He hauled out a dark green plastic bag stuffed full of a week's accumulation of trash and garbage. I was immediately grateful that we'd eaten most of our meals in restaurants. We had, however, cooked fish one evening and the smell of the three-day-old remnants dominated the air around the bag.

"Dump it out," Dave said. "We've got to find that chart."

"Yes, sir," Al said as he worked to pry open the knot at the top.

"Another high point in the vacation I'll never forget," I said as the mess spilled out onto the six-foot-square concrete slab at the bottom of the back steps. Dave looked like he didn't know whether to laugh or cry, so I decided for him by forcing a burst of laughter. We were all in need of that.

Breathing shallowly, we got down on our knees and began to pick prissily through the smelly mass. Soon we were accompanied by a swarm of houseflies and a trio of yellow jacket wasps that found the odor more attractive than we did. We all exhaled with vigor and retreated from the pile when Al announced that he had found the envelope.

Daffy Dolly had dropped the sack from the bathroom into the big green garbage bag before depositing the larger, juicier collection of goodies from the kitchen. The trickle-down effect left the treasure chart stained with drippings from some grapefruit rinds that had been ripening in the kitchen waste.

"This lends an air of authenticity to our map," Al said as he sniffed at the chart and wrinkled his nose.

"We won't breathe easy until we've cracked the code," I said.

"Maybe we can just follow our noses to the treasure," he said.

Al, Dave and I completed the unpleasant task by scooping the mess back into the barrel and replacing the lid, trapping half a dozen persistent flies inside. The disappointed yellow jackets circled the closed container for a minute before zooming off in search of more accessible goodies.

When the three of us got back into the house, the sound of running water told us that both showers were occupied. Given the option of joining their wives in the showers or waiting it out with me on the porch, Dave and Al made the obvious choice. Thus, I was left all by myself to think about a new hiding place for the chart.

My first move was to limit the odor of overripe grapefruit emanating from the chart by sealing it in a plastic zipper bag. Next, I stuffed this package into a small, brown paper sack I pulled out of a stash of second-hand containers in the kitchen. The question remained: where could I hide it from treasure hunters and trash haulers?

My train of thought was derailed by Cindy, who walked barefoot onto the porch clad in a white terrycloth robe and announced that the upstairs shower would be available in a minute, as soon as Dave's feet were dry. I thanked her and presented her with the brown paper bag.

"I've got the perfect place for this," she said. "Follow me."

Cindy led me into the kitchen, where she opened the freezer compartment at the top of the refrigerator and slid the package into the back. She moved a gallon of ice cream and the remains of a five-pound bag of ice over in front of the brown bag and closed the door. "I don't think Daffy Dolly does freezers," she said.

"It'll be safe in there from Al and Dave, but you'd better warn Carol," I said before heading toward the stairs. "She's been known to clean things up and throw things out at her house."

I finished my shower and was pulling on a clean T-shirt when my cell phone rang. I dashed across the room and snatched the phone off the dresser. Did the catnapper have my cell phone number? No, he didn't. Caller ID told me it was Martha Todd.

"Did you get Sherlock back okay?" she asked as soon as I said hello.

"All I got was a lump on my head," I said, and poured out the details of the previous night's fiasco.

"I wish I was there to massage your poor head," Martha said when I stopped to take a breath.

"I wish you were here to massage my poor head and every other part of my poor body," I said.

"Will you be able to give that bastard the code he wants?"

"We're pretty sure the code died with the guy who made it up. But we've got a plan for catching said bastard and forcing him to give back Sherlock." I told her what we had in mind for this evening and Martha said it sounded like a winner.

"It can't miss," I said. "I'll call you tomorrow and let you talk to Sherlock in person." Martha laughed and we made the usual kissy sounds before saying goodnight.

★ ★ ★

The kitchen phone rang at 11:31 p.m. I picked it up and said, "Hello, asshole."

"Sticks and stones, pussy lover," Falsetto Voice said. "You got something to write with?"

"Yes," I said. Walt kept a pad and a handful of ballpoint pens beside the phone.

"Okay. Go to Waban Park, the end away from the water. There's a new plaque there that says it's in memory of Alley somebody, but everybody still calls it Waban Park. Call this number and I'll tell you where to bring the code." He recited the number and hung up. Apparently Falsetto Voice believed the house phone was bugged and was circumventing the bug by forcing me to use my cell phone for directions to the meeting place. This would actually work to my advantage because I didn't want the cops around either.

I was alone in the house, my four companions having departed earlier to avoid being seen if Falsetto Voice was watching for my exit. Using my cell phone, I called Al's cell and then Dave's to tell them where I was going before I went out the front door.

Waban Park was only about a block-and-a-half away. It was a one-block-wide rectangular park that extended inland two blocks from Beach Road, which was the road overlooking the Oak Bluffs town beach and Nantucket Sound. The park was a motley patch of grass that offered nothing in the way of amenities or attractions. The only activity we'd seen there when we drove past was a golfer practicing his nine-iron shots, a woman with a plastic bag picking up after her dog and a solitary Canada goose nibbling at the grass.

With a white envelope bearing a phony code in my right hand and my flashlight in the left, I walked slowly to the park. I wanted to give my troops time to get into position in case Falsetto Voice was planning to make his move there instead of directing me to another meeting place.

I reached the inland end of the park and kept walking along the edge until I was about halfway across. I'd written the number I was supposed to call on the envelope, which I held half-wrapped around the flashlight while pulling out my cell phone. I was attempting to hold the envelope and the cell phone in my right hand and read the number with the flashlight I had in my left hand when a male voice barked, "Hold it right there."

I turned my head and saw the shadowy outline of a man who'd moved silently up behind me. Before I could pivot and bring the flashlight to bear on his face I heard him grunt and yell, "What the hell?" as a paint ball fired by Al hit him in the back, just above the waist.

When the man whipped around to face his attacker, I dropped the phone and the envelope and pulled a paintball pistol out of my waistband. I fired and saw a yellow splotch appear between his shoulder blades.

"Son of a bitch!" the man screamed as he spun to face me. I directed the flashlight into his face and my knees buckled when I saw who I'd shot.

CHAPTER 12

MISTAKEN IDENTITY

"What the fuck are you doin'?" yelled Detective Manny Gouveia.

"Hold your fire," I yelled, but not in time to stop another paint ball from smacking the detective squarely in the butt. "Stop," I yelled again. "It's the cops."

My four companions, all dressed in black, emerged from the shadows, along with three additional police officers. My knees were shaking and I could barely hold onto the flashlight by the time the circle of stunned observers surrounding Manny and me was completed.

The paint-splattered detective aimed a flashlight into my face, blinding me. "Like I said, what the fuck are you doin'?" he said.

I was unable to speak, but Al managed to say that he'd thought Manny was the guy who'd stolen the cat, and that he was very sorry about the paintballs.

"Me, too," I finally said in a voice an octave higher than normal. Manny lowered the flashlight beam, but all I could see for the next several minutes was the residual ball of reverse light.

"Let me get this straight," Manny said. "You people were gonna bomb this guy, the guy who might have murdered a man, with paintballs?"

"You got it," Dave said. "We were going to surround him and capture him with the paintball guns."

"Did you not consider the fact that we had your phone tapped and would be here?" Manny asked.

"We were hoping to grab the bastard before you guys could get here," Dave said.

"Jesus H. Christ," Manny said. "What do they put in the water in Minnesota? Whose dingbat idea was this?"

"It was mine," Dave said.

"What are you? A fugitive from a Minnesota nut house?" Manny asked.

"He's a cartoonist," I said.

"Oh, well, that explains it," Manny said. "This paintball posse is right out of the fuckin' funny papers."

"I know it sounds crazy," Dave said. "But these were the only weapons we could buy without a permit."

"It not only sounds crazy, it is crazy," Manny said. "How'd you all like to be charged with assaulting an officer?"

"Please," I said. "It was a mistake. It was dark and we thought you were the catnapper."

"Like I should give a shit what you thought?" Manny said. "You could have hurt me bad if you'd hit my face. You wrecked my goddamn clothes."

Carol Jeffrey stepped forward. "We'll pay for your clothes," she said. "We'll buy you anything you want, but please don't arrest us. We should all be chasing the cat thief, not fighting with each other."

In silence, the detective studied us, moving the flashlight from one contrite face to another, for what seemed like an hour. "Call the number he gave you," he said when his flashlight came around to me.

I retrieved the envelope and my cell phone from the grass,

and with Manny shining his light on my hand, I punched in the number. Falsetto Voice answered on the third ring.

"You stupid asshole," he said. "I watched you shoot that cop with fuckin' paintballs. I ain't laughed so hard since my little sister pissed in her pants on the Ferris wheel and it dripped on some people down below."

"Where do you want to meet me?" I asked.

"Nowhere tonight," he said. "And maybe nowhere ever. Maybe I'll get the code somewhere else and you can kiss your pussycat good-bye." He was laughing when he punched off his phone, but it registered on the tatters of my brain that his last words hadn't been spoken in falsetto—and the gravelly voice was vaguely familiar.

I repeated Falsetto Voice's words and everybody, including the cops, groaned.

"I guess he's had enough of you clowns," Manny said. "And I can't say that I blame him."

"I swear I've heard that voice before," I said. "If I could just remember where...."

"Well, if you do, the first person you tell is me," Manny said. "This is police business and I don't want no more of this do-it-yourself crap, do you understand me?"

We all said we did.

"You damn well better," he said. "Next time, you're all goin' in front of a judge on a charge of interferin' with an officer. Good night now."

We all said goodnight as Manny started to walk away. After a couple of steps, he turned back and said, "You'll be gettin' my bill for new clothes."

"We'll be happy to pay it," I said. Under the circumstances, this was God's truth.

The paintball army retreated slowly back to its bivouac at the cottage, where we stowed our weapons in a box under the stairs. Carol and Cindy said goodnight and went to their bedrooms. Al, Dave and I gathered on the porch for a debriefing.

"Shit," Al said.

"That's my feeling exactly," Dave said.

"Me, too," I said.

"You've got to remember where you heard that voice," Al said. "Otherwise, Sherlock's in big trouble."

I had been replaying the sound in my head without results. "Maybe if I sleep on, it the answer will pop into my head by morning," I said.

"Leave some space open for it to pop into," Dave said.

"He's got no problem finding open space," Al said.

When I finally spaced out, my dreams were filled with falsetto commands, flying paintballs and furry cats running away from fierce pursuers. Just before waking, I heard the gravelly voice and a face flashed through the final seconds of the dream.

I sat up shouting, "I know who you are." Apparently nobody heard me, so I said it again in a normal tone. Still wearing the scarlet pajamas I'd bought especially for this trip (at home I don't bother with PJ's), I ran down to the kitchen, looked up the Oak Bluffs police number, called the station and asked for Detective Gouveia.

"He doesn't come in on Saturday, sir," said the officer who answered. "And if he did, it wouldn't be until 8 o'clock." I looked at the clock on the kitchen wall and discovered it was 5:48 a.m.

"Sorry," I said. "But I really need to talk to him. Could you please contact him at a more reasonable hour and have him call Mitch Mitchell? You can tell him it's about the catnapper."

There was a moment of silence before the officer responded. "Very well, sir. Give me your number and I'll call the detective at nine."

I gave him the numbers of the house phone and my cell phone and hung up. When I turned around, I found myself facing a man with a gun pointed at my belly.

"Don't shoot, Al," I said. "I've had a flash of recollection."

"They say two aspirins can cure those flashes," he said. "What the hell are you doing down here at this hour?"

"I was using the phone," I said. "Why are you standing there half-naked with a paintball gun in your hands?" He was wearing only the bottom half of a pair of black-and-white striped shorty pajamas.

"I thought you might be the catnapper sneaking in here to hunt for the code. I was hoping to paint him red."

"Sorry to dampen your artistic ardor, but I can make up for it by telling you who I think the catnapper is."

Al showed little surprise when I named my suspect. He put the gun away and we both went back to bed, but I was too wound up for sleep. At 6:30, I gave up, got up and picked up my cell phone. It would be 10:30 on Saturday morning in Cape Verde, a good time to call Martha.

It turned out not to be such a good time. I got her answering machine and left a message saying things had gone slightly awry with our foolproof Friday night plan but that we'd be rescuing Sherlock for sure today. I didn't ask where she was and who she was with, but I was hoping it wasn't a late breakfast with a friend named Frederico.

The hammering in my head had gone away during the night, so I volunteered to bike to the bakery on Healey Square to pick up some goodies for breakfast. I had just locked my bike into the rack at the square when Daffy Dolly emerged from the bakery. Her bike, which she hadn't locked, was propped against a bench a few feet from the bakery door.

Wondering if she knew where Walt had gone, I tried to intercept her. She saw me, paused for a moment, and then practically ran for her bike.

"Dolly, please," I said. "I need to talk to you."

Without looking back, she got on the bike and pedaled away. By the time I could have detached my bike from the rack, she'd have been so far ahead that I couldn't have followed her if I'd wanted to. And I definitely did not want to go pedaling after Dolly again.

We ate sticky buns, bagels and apple fritters and drank two pots of coffee while waiting on the porch for Manny Gouveia to call. We were talking about reloading the paintball guns and taking matters into our own hands again when the kitchen phone finally rang at a few minutes before 11 a.m.

"I been out buyin' clothes," Manny said. "What's on your mind?"

"The catnapper," I said. "I'm pretty sure I know who it is. Let's talk about catching him this morning."

"It's Saturday, Mr. Mitchell. I ain't on duty today."

"You said to call you when I remembered the voice. If we don't get him today, he might do what he's threatened to do with my cat. I'm taking action, whether you help me or not."

"You ain't goin' nowhere near that guy without police backup. Sit your ass down on the porch and I'll be right over. Oh, and get your checkbook out—I'm bringin' the bill for my new pants and shirt and underwear."

"Underwear?"

"Yeah, underwear. The paint went all the way through my pants and I ain't walkin' around with a red spot on my ass, even if nobody sees it."

Manny drove up in his island pickup about 10 minutes later. Like Al, he showed little surprise when I named my suspect. In turn, I expressed considerable surprise when I saw the bill for his clothing.

"Where'd you shop, Niemann-Marcus?" I asked.

"Island prices, Mr. Mitchell," he said. "Island prices."

I wrote him a check and we all discussed strategy for an assault on Falsetto Voice. We agreed to act quickly and set H-Hour for 30 minutes past high noon.

CHAPTER 13

RAIDERS OF THE ARK

The five of us walked to the Oak Bluffs harbor, where we found a large and loud collection of Saturday boaters and ferry-borne day-trippers filling the sidewalk and the open air restaurants. These visitors had a perfect day for their fun, with the temperature in the low 80s and the sky displaying a scattering of white puffy clouds to accentuate the blue.

"Think we'll draw a crowd?" Al asked as we wound our way toward our target through the mob of people dressed in various combinations of shorts, tank tops and swimsuits. The smells of sweaty bodies, sunscreen and fried clams mingled and drifted in the air.

"People will probably think we're shooting a movie or a TV show," I said. "'Pirates of the Caribbean Invade Martha's Vineyard.'"

"With all these extras, we've got plenty of cover while we're moving in," Dave said.

The blacktop sidewalk next to the water was bordered on the inland side by a knee-high metal rail. A row of rental cars was backed up against the rail and we took our designated positions behind a couple of the rental cars at 12:25. I looked around for our police backup and spotted one officer in uniform crouching behind a six-foot-high stack of lobster traps beside the sidewalk.

At 12:30 sharp, I took out my cell phone and dialed the number that Falsetto Voice had given me the previous evening. We watched as "Cap'n" Charles Morgan, who sat eating a pizza and drinking beer on the afterdeck of the All That Glitters, picked up his cell phone.

I heard him say, "Yeah?" with both ears—the one open toward the boat and the one pressed against my phone.

"Look around you on the dock, asshole," I said into the phone.

Morgan looked up and saw Manny Gouveia and two uniformed cops step out from behind their respective hiding places. The officers moved toward the All That Glitters and the five of us also closed in.

"Request permission to come aboard," I said into the phone.

"Come aboard and kiss my ass," Morgan said. "Your gangbuster buddies better have a warrant." He snapped his phone shut, put it down and stood up to face Manny, who was stepping onto the deck with a search warrant in his outstretched right hand.

"Just what do you think you're lookin' for?" Morgan asked as Manny presented the warrant.

"We think you might have something onboard that belongs to Mr. Mitchell here," Manny said.

"And what would that be?" Morgan asked.

"My cat," I said. "Where is he?"

"Don't know what you're talkin' about," Morgan said. "I got no use for cats on my boat."

"You're right about that," I said. "Rats generally don't care for cats."

"The warrant also allows us to search for a certain chart that was taken from Mr. Mitchell by force," Manny said to Morgan.

"Have a seat and finish your lunch while we take a look around. Officer Silva here will keep you company."

Morgan grunted and looked at officer Silva, who stood about six-three, weighed around 240 and carried a nine-millimeter police special in the holster on his right hip. With no further prompting, Morgan sat down and took a quick swig from his bottle of beer.

I followed Manny and the other officer down a ladder into the living quarters of the All That Glitters. The spaces below deck were surprisingly uncluttered considering the scruffy appearance of the boat's current resident. I called Sherlock's name over and over as we moved through the vessel.

We checked two sleeping compartments without finding as much as a cat hair. Manny combed through a small desk in one of the compartments, but didn't find the chart. The head was empty, and so was the galley. On a whim, I looked into the small refrigerator. On the bottom shelf was an open can of cat food.

"We're getting warm," I said, pointing out my find to Manny. "We could take this can up topside and wave it under Morgan's nose until he talks."

"That'll be our trump card if we need it," he said. "Let's try the engine room."

The temperature of the stale air in the engine room was at least 100 degrees. I hoped that Sherlock wasn't in that pressure cooker, but I called his name again. For once I was glad to get no response.

"Now what?" I said when we were back in the passageway.

"There's some storage lockers way up in the bow," Manny said. "I saw them when we searched this tub for some sign of where Wade Waters might have gone after he disappeared."

Forward we went and again I hollered, "Sherlock." This time my reward was a muffled meow.

The sound came from behind a three-foot-high metal locker door. The latch was secured with a padlock. Manny sent the officer, whose name was O'Connor, up to get Charles Morgan's keys. O'Connor returned quickly with a heavy assortment on a steel ring. It took Manny less than a minute to find the right one. The lock popped open, Manny yanked it off and I opened the locker door, releasing an odor that indicated an urgent need for fresh kitty litter.

On the floor sat my cat carrier with my cat's nose pressed tight against the gate. A second later the gate was open, Sherlock Holmes was in my arms and we were headed up the ladder to fresh air and sunshine. Manny was right behind me, followed by Officer O'Connor holding the cat carrier at arm's length.

"Look what we found," I said as I stepped onto the deck. Immediately, I was surrounded by Al, Carol, Dave and Cindy, all trying to pet Sherlock, who flattened his ears and endured the flood of attention.

"He looks pretty good for a hostage," Al said.

"He seems to have had food and water, but his litter box is toxic." The small pan, kept in the carrier for emergencies, was loaded far beyond capacity.

Manny Gouveia strode toward Morgan, who slowly rose from his chair. "So, are you satisfied, detective?" he asked.

"Almost," said Manny. "I'll be more satisfied when you're in a cell. Charles Morgan, you're under arrest for breaking and entering and theft of an animal. You have the right to remain silent—"

Morgan cut him off in mid-rights. "Is that all the charges you got?" he asked as Officer Silva cuffed his hands behind his back.

"That's all for now but we'll find some more," Manny said. "If we locate that chart aboard this boat, we can also stick you with the theft of that, plus assault and battery on Mr. Mitchell. And unless you suddenly produce the friend you were supposedly havin' a drink with the day your partner died, it kind of looks like we could add murder to the list."

"I didn't kill nobody," Morgan said. "No matter what else you think I did, I didn't kill nobody."

"We'll let the court decide about that," Manny said. "Right now, let's take a ride to the station."

The sight of three police officers boarding the boat had attracted a mob of rubber-neckers, some of whom were almost falling off the dock trying to get a closer look at the action on the All That Glitters. Like Moses parting the Red Sea, Officers Silva and O'Connor cleared a path and Manny marched his captive through the gap to a cruiser in the nearby parking lot.

"Thanks, detective," I yelled as they walked away.

"Have a good day," Manny said. "And try not to call me again on a Saturday."

Our little group of five (six, counting Sherlock Holmes) could have used a police escort to help us get off the boat. The crowd closed ranks around the All That Glitters and we had to push our way onto the dock. Questioning faces pressed uncomfortably close to ours and questioning voices melded into an undecipherable cacophony as we waded through the human sea. Sherlock Holmes began to squirm nervously in my arms and, for a moment, I was afraid I'd have to put him back into the reeking cat carrier.

Sherlock's front claws were digging deep into my right biceps when we finally broke free by dashing across Lake Avenue in front of a bus that blocked our tormentors long enough to discourage further pursuit. When I persuaded Sherlock to withdraw his weapons, drops of blood seeped out of the puncture wounds in my bare arm.

Carol noticed the dots of red. "Poor kitty was scared to death," she said.

"And poor Mitchy will need a transfusion," I said.

"Have you suffered catastrophic wounds?" Al asked.

"I could catalog them for you," I said. "I'm feline like I've been stabbed."

When we were halfway through Ocean Park, the cell phone in my pocket sounded off. I transferred the bundle in my arms to Al and pulled out the phone.

It was Martha. "Have you got Sherlock yet?"

"Safe and sound," I said. "I had him in my arms when the phone rang."

"Let me talk to him." I put the phone next to Sherlock's left ear, which still lay flat against his skull. I heard Martha's voice and watched as the ear flicked up. Martha kept talking, but she couldn't coax an answering meow.

"He's being strong and silent," I said, reclaiming use of the phone. "But he looked happy to hear from you." I went on to describe the rescue and the struggle with the curious crowd.

"Well, now that you've got him back, take better care of him," Martha said.

"I wish I was taking him back to St. Paul tomorrow," I said. "But we're stuck here, supposedly having fun, until next Sunday. I just hope nobody else comes looking for that chart."

"Me, too. For your sake as well as Sherlock's."

"With Morgan in jail, we should be safe." We chatted some more, just long enough for me to find out that Martha had gone out for breakfast with a group of people from the attorney general's office.

"Would you believe Frederico picked up the tab?" she said.

I'd believe anything she said about that show-off. "That's nice," I said. "What was the occasion?"

"His divorce became final yesterday," Martha said. "He's now officially a free man and Cape Verde's most eligible bachelor."

Just what I wanted to hear. Frederico now had three-and-a-half months of official bachelorhood to worm himself deeper into Martha's life.

"You don't look happy," Al said when I took back my cat. "You've got your pussycat back, why aren't you smiling?"

"It's the pussy chaser in Cape Verde that's bothering me," I said. "Pretty boy Frederico's divorce is now final and you know which pussy he'll be going after."

After returning Sherlock Holmes to his rightful place on my bed, I stuffed the litter box and its contents into the outdoor trash barrel. As I closed the lid, I was grateful that the litter box hadn't been in the barrel when we dug through everything in search of the missing chart.

Cindy made a platter of sandwiches and dumped a bag of chips into a bowl, and we ate a late lunch on the porch. While the others debated which beach to loaf on during the remainder of the afternoon, I biked to Circuit Avenue and bought a replacement for the cat carrier litter box at the hardware store. One never knows when such an item might be needed on the long trip back to St. Paul at the end of this never-to-be-forgotten vacation.

I hosed out the cat carrier and left it on the back patio to dry prior to installing the new litter box. When I joined the crew on the porch, intending to ask about the remaining plan of the day, Dave was grinning and folding up his cell phone.

"Guess what?" Dave said. "We're going to a party tonight."

"Where?" Cindy asked.

"Why?" Al asked.

"Whose?" Carol asked.

"That was Harry Dick," Dave said. "He's got me a contract with a syndicate that's going to place my cartoons in 250 papers and he's throwing a party to celebrate."

After a raucous round of hallelujahs, hugs and high-fives, Cindy asked where the party was being held. Dave said it would be at the bed-and-breakfast in Chilmark where Harry was staying. "I wrote down the directions. He guessed it would take us about half an hour to get there. He wants us there by 6:30 for cocktails and, as he said it, horse's doovers."

Cindy asked the question that always seems to be uppermost in the female mind. "What are we supposed to wear?"

"He didn't say anything about that," Dave said.

"Just like a man," Cindy said. "And you didn't ask, also just like a man."

"He did say it's going to be outdoors by the swimming pool, if that helps. Sounds like they're grilling some kind of fish out there."

"Guess we won't need to rent tuxes," Al said.

"Do we have to wear ties with our T-shirts?" I asked.

"Not in that neck of the woods," Al said.

★ ★ ★

Not knowing whether to be on time or fashionably late, we opted for promptness and left Oak Bluffs a few minutes before 6. The women were dressed almost like twins in V-neck blouses, slacks and sandals. We men were wearing newly-purchased Martha's Vineyard T-shirts (mine featured a cartoon shark rising open-mouthed toward a swimmer who was ogling a mermaid reclining on a rock), khaki shorts and sandals. The height of island fashion.

Harry Dick's directions took us through an intersection near the Vineyard Haven harbor where the traffic was so grid-locked that we could have made better time walking. After we finally untied that Gordian knot, we drove through several miles of semi-open country, where the woods and fields were interspersed with shops and tourist attractions. We were instructed to follow the sign to Menemsha, which pointed to the right a few yards past the biggest oak tree any of us had ever seen, with ground-level branches that spread out like a giant, leafy octopus. A couple of miles after the turn we saw a sign that said Summer Sweet on the left side of the road.

"This is it," Dave said. "I hope they'll let us in with this rusted-out wreck we're driving."

"It's an island car," Al said. "They'll welcome us as natives."

Dave turned into the smoothly-graded gravel driveway and eventually we were met by a young man wearing a bright blue T-shirt with a white Summer Sweet logo. He pointed us toward a parking place among the trees, Dave parked the car and we piled out to have a look at the amenities of Summer Sweet.

In the center of the complex was a large, three-story, Victorian house painted in three shades of gray with black and white trim. Around it on three sides were several smaller dwellings of similar style that looked like single or double units. In back of the smaller units was the pool, surrounded by a patio the size of a baseball diamond.

On the patio, we saw a group of people with drinks in their hands. As we approached, two individuals emerged from the gathering and came to greet us. One was Harry Dick, whose bare belly protruded through a floral-patterned, unbuttoned, short-sleeve shirt and hung over the waistband of a normal-length, tiger-striped swimsuit. I breathed a silent word of gratitude that he wasn't wearing the Speedo.

Our other greeter was Rhonda Fairchild, whose tangerine bikini left little to the imagination—not that I needed to use any imagination after our previous meeting on the beach. She still wore the shiny bauble in her bellybutton.

Harry shook hands all around, but Rhonda greeted me with a hug, somehow managing not to spill anything from her half-full glass while wrapping both arms around my neck.

"You and me are going to have a real good time tonight," Rhonda whispered. Her breath was warm and moist in my ear and her breasts, only the tips of which were encumbered by the bikini top, were pressed firmly against my chest. Out of the corner of my eye, I saw Carol frown.

CHAPTER 14

PARTY TIME

With Rhonda holding my hand, I managed to stay with the group as our host, Harry Dick, led us around and introduced us to some of the other guests.

One who stood out was a tall, lean, white-haired man in a red polo shirt and white shorts with a pressed-in crease. His name was Henry Agnew. He grasped Dave's right hand firmly in both of his, congratulated Dave effusively and said, "Bring your wife and your friends with you to Edgartown, and I'll give you all a free ride."

"A free ride in what?" Dave asked.

"On one of my catamarans," Agnew said. "I run a fleet of catamarans and sail boats, for which I charge outrageous prices to people looking for a real sea-going adventure. If you want speed, my cats will hit 50 knots when the wind is right. And if you want romance, we have a cocktail cruise every evening from Edgartown to Menemsha, where the sunsets are spectacular."

"Sounds like fun," Dave said. "We might just take you up on that romantic sunset cruise."

"Here's my card," Agnew said. "Just give me a call by noon on the day you want to ride so I can save five life jackets for you."

"You can make that four," I said. "I don't ride on anything

smaller than the Steamship Authority ferry."

"There's nothing safer than my catamaran," Agnew said. "You couldn't tip it over if you tried."

"It's just that I have a problem with this particular body of water," I said.

"Somebody tried to drown Mitch out there the last time he was on the Vineyard," Dave said. "We'll hogtie him and bring him along and make sure he has fun."

"I can keep him company on shore," Rhonda said. "I don't need to be on a boat to have fun with a guy like Mitch." She squeezed my hand and snuggled her velvety cheek against mine.

"I'm surprised you came back to the island after an experience like that," Agnew said. His eyes kept slipping away from my face to ogle Rhonda's tits.

"Dave was very persuasive and I wanted to meet his uncle, Walter Jerome," I said. "I suppose you know him."

"Oh, sure," Agnew said. "I've advertised in what used to be Walt's paper practically all my life. I really miss having him there."

"Well, I guess he's happy doing freelance," I said. "Did you read the magazine piece he did on the treasure hunter they fished out of water last week? Wade Waters?"

"No," he said. "Can't say that I did. I don't have much interest in the kind of people who waste their lives hunting for sunken treasure ships."

"I read that Waters was originally from the Vineyard," I said. "I thought maybe you'd know him."

"I'd met him sometime or other, but I can't say I knew him. Like I said, I don't have much interest in treasure hunters."

Our conversation was interrupted by Rhonda, who tugged on my right arm and said it was time to refill her glass. "You need something, too," she said as she ordered a gin and tonic at the portable bar.

"Ginger ale," I said to the bartender. "On the rocks."

"What kind of pussy drink is that?" Rhonda asked, taking a generous gulp of her gin concoction.

"It's an alcoholic's pussy drink," I said. "One sip of what you're drinking and I'd be off on a drunk that would leave me laying flat on my face in a puddle of puke."

"Eew! You sure know how to make a girl feel good."

"I suspect you'll be feeling very good when you finish that one."

"I suspect you'll be feeling good, too, after we've had supper because then you'll be feeling me." She punctuated this with a giggle.

"In that case, I'll be looking forward to dessert." I was wondering how far this could go with Carol keeping an eye on me.

Rhonda towed me to the hors d'oeuvres table, where we found three kinds of cheese, assorted crackers, chicken wings, pizza rolls, plain chips, chips with ridges, an assortment of dips and a platter filled with little raw clams on the half shell. "Have a cherrystone," she said, picking up a clam and aiming it toward my mouth.

"No thanks," I said, putting up a hand to block the incoming missile. "I prefer my food to be dead."

"You really are a pussy," Rhonda said. She turned the shell toward her mouth and slurped the cold, wet morsel. "Haven't you ever heard the old saying about when in Rome eat what the Romans eat?"

"The Romans can have my share of those." I put chunks of cheese on a trio of crackers and crunched into the first one.

A flash of light hit our faces and I looked up to see a man pointing a camera at us. After another flash, he approached us, introduced himself as Don Streeter and said he was a photographer for the *Gazette*.

"This party is worthy of pix in the *Gazette*?" I said.

"Oh, yeah," he said. "Harry can be a loudmouthed pain in the ass, but as an agent he represents a lot of important people. When he has a party, some big names show up."

"Like who?"

"Like Carly Simon, who's right over there," he said, pointing to a tall brunette who was chatting with a familiar-looking man. "And of course, that's Ted Danson she's talking to."

Suddenly, I was more impressed with the loudmouthed pain in the ass who had become Dave's agent.

Streeter asked me what my name was and what I was doing on the island and I found myself spilling out my whole story about wanting to meet Walter Jerome and inadvertently getting involved in the search for Wade Waters's treasure map. Rhonda finished her drink, went to the bar and came back with a fresh one while I was telling my tale.

"Jeez, if you're interested in Wade Waters and his life as a treasure hunter you should talk to Terry Shaw at the *Gazette*," Streeter said when I finally finished my story. "She's been writing about everything that floats around the island for probably 40 years."

"Maybe I'll do that," I said. "Seeing as how Waters's partner made things personal by stealing my cat." Walt Jerome's story about Waters had concentrated on the search for the Daniel French, with only a brief mention of Waters's island background. A little history lesson might be interesting—and it might provide a clue to breaking the code on the chart.

When Streeter moved away to get a close-up shot of Carly Simon talking to our host, Rhonda stretched up and kissed my right ear lobe. Rhonda's breath made me wonder if I could get drunk from the gin fumes and I was pulling my ear away from her cold, wet lips when Harry began shouting for attention.

"Okay, everybody," Harry said when babble ceased. "Horse's doovers are over and it's time to put on the feed bag for the piece dee resistance. Line your butts up behind our guest of honor, Mr. David Jerome, and his lovely wife, Cindy, grab yourself a plate and load up with goodies."

Harry waved Dave toward the end of a long table lined with aluminum caterer's pans. A row of young women wearing well-filled Summer Sweet T-shirts stood behind the table dishing out the food—grilled swordfish, rice pilaf, roasted carrots, green salad and rolls. Rhonda released my earlobe voluntarily, pushed me into line and stepped in behind me. She followed so close that her boobs were bumping against my back every time I stopped moving and I began to worry about her bikini top sliding off.

"Don't you want to cover up a bit?" I asked over my shoulder. "The mosquitoes will eat you up with all that skin exposed."

"Mosquitoes?" she said. "Are you kidding? They spray this place until every bug within five miles drops dead. Actually, I'd take off everything if they'd let me do that out here."

I looked around, wondering if Carol was observing the action, and was grateful to see her picking up a dinner plate with her back toward me.

As a precautionary measure, I stepped back and eased myself back into line behind Rhonda. "Ladies first," I said, and she giggled.

We reached the end of the table, moved along and got our food without further danger of a wardrobe malfunction.

"Your friends over there want us to sit with them," Rhonda said as we emerged from the serving line. Sure enough, Al and Carol had saved chairs for us at a small folding table and were waving for us to join them.

"Do me a favor and don't get too cuddly at the table," I said as we walked toward the Jeffreys. "Carol is Norwegian and she's kind of prudish about public displays of affection." *Especially when it's not Martha in the display*, I added to myself.

"Okay, I'll control my natural urges while we're with them, but it won't be easy," Rhonda said. "You feel so strong and sexy it's hard to keep my hands off of you."

"Flattery will get you everywhere."

"That's good because I'm planning to get everywhere with you right after dinner."

We put our plates down, and I plopped into a chair while Rhonda went off to get a glass of wine. As I watched her bobbing bikini bottom roll away, I noticed that she wasn't walking a straight line.

"That young lady seems to know you pretty well," Carol said.

"She was with Harry on the beach the day Dave met with him," I said. "She's from Minnesota, so she's interested in talking about home."

"And it looks like she's making herself very much at home with you," Carol said.

Rhonda returned before I could say anything in defense of my virtue. She made no physical contact while we ate, except for an occasional squeeze of my thigh under the table, and the dinner conversation was light and pleasant. When we'd finished, Harry Dick rose from his seat between Dave and Cindy and announced that he had procured some after-dinner entertainment for our listening pleasure. He introduced an island blue-grass band, which set up near the pool and launched into a medley of tunes.

Carol excused herself to go to the ladies room and Al strolled over to join Harry and the Jeromes. Rhonda dragged me to the bar to procure another glass of wine. She was holding my arm so tight and leaning so heavily against me for support that I suggested maybe she didn't need anything more to drink.

She laughed and asked the bartender for a glass of merlot.

With the fresh drink in hand, she said, "Now it's dark enough for me to show you my room." Still holding my arm in a strangulation grip, she steered me toward the main house.

"What do you mean dark enough?" I asked, although I thought I knew the answer.

"Don't you remember? Us Lindstrom girls only screw in the dark."

Okay. That was the answer I'd been expecting.

As I opened the front door, I looked around, searching for Carol. I was feeling as sneaky as I did when I was a little boy slipping away from my parents to have a cigarette behind the barn. Rhonda gave a tug on my arm, yanked me through the doorway and towed me down the hall. I hadn't seen Carol, and I hoped Carol hadn't seen me.

"Hold this," Rhonda said, handing me the glass of wine. Still clinging to my arm with her left hand, she fished her electronic key out of her bikini bottom with her right hand.

She waved the piece of plastic past my face. "Want to see where this came from?" she asked. Giggling, she tried to slide the card into the slot beside the lock. I say tried because it took her three attempts to line the key up with the opening.

The door finally opened and we went in to find the room illuminated only by the last rays of the setting sun shining through a large window. I could see the outlines but not the details of the furnishings, which I imagined were as plush as the accommodations I'd seen around the pool.

Rhonda reclaimed her wine, took a gulp from the glass and set it on a nightstand beside the bed. When she turned to face me, her bikini top was already gone. A second later, the bottom was on the floor at her feet and I was again looking at the woman I'd seen on the beach wearing nothing but a gleaming stud in her bellybutton.

"Time to get naked, big boy," she said, spreading her arms like wings. The motion caused her to sway at a precarious angle, so I grasped her outspread hands and, pressing full-length against her naked body, pushed her gently backward until her legs touched the bed.

"Maybe you'd better lie down," I said.

"Good idea," Rhonda said. She flopped straight back and lay crosswise on the bed, with her legs dangling and her toes brushing the floor. I picked up her ankles, turned her body 90 degrees and swung her feet up onto the bed. She promptly spread her legs into an inviting V, with the land of enchantment at the tip of her short-hair spear faintly visible in the fast-fading light.

"Get naked, close the drapes so it's really dark and come and get the girl from Lindstrom," she said in a soft, dreamy voice.

"I need to use your bathroom first," I said. "I'll be right back."

"Don't be gone long," Rhonda said. "I'm all ready for you."

I needed time in the bathroom to think as well as to pee. My problems were threefold: First, I was being nagged by a growing sense of guilt. How could I square my romping with Rhonda with my concern about the possibility of Martha Todd frolicking with Frederico?

Second, Rhonda had reached a level of inebriation that was obliterating her judgment. Would she wake up in the morning with no memory of her enticements and complain that I'd forced her to have sex?

Third, when Harry's party ended, my traveling companions would be looking for me. Would Carol rat me out to Martha if they found me in Rhonda's room?

Still fully-clothed and wondering how the hell I was going to handle this situation, I went back into the bedroom. The sunlight was gone and the room was almost dark. Rhonda still lay on her back with her legs spread, leaving the gates of heaven open and available at the point of the spear. From her mouth came a soft sound, but it wasn't a whisper of invitation. It was a snore.

On the top shelf of the closet, I found a blanket. Gently, I spread it over the gorgeous body on the bed. Ever so carefully, I tipped her head forward far enough to slide a pillow underneath. I took the wine glass off the nightstand, dumped what was left down the bathroom sink and set the glass gently down on the dresser.

I opened the door without a sound, slid out into the hall and eased the door shut so softly that the latch barely clicked. As I turned toward the main entrance, I came within inches of banging into one Alan Jeffrey and barely stifled a yelp of surprise that might have penetrated the unconscious brain of the sleeping beauty.

"Harry said I'd find you in this room," Al said. "How was it?"

"It wasn't," I said. "The lady passed out."

"Oh, come now!"

"No, I didn't come now. You saw how drunk she was getting."

"So what are you going to tell Carol, who was sure I'd be interrupting you in the throes of mad, passionate love?"

"I'll tell her the truth—that I escorted a rather tipsy lady to her room and left her to sleep off an overdose of gin mixed with merlot."

"Off the record, was the tipsy lady's bikini still on when you left?"

"Off the record, a gentleman never discusses how a recumbent lady was dressed."

"I'll take that answer as a 'no,'" Al said.

Carol looked at me accusingly when Al and I joined the trio at the car. The accusation turned to skepticism when I described my gentlemanly conduct—a description that ended with my ushering Rhonda into her room, seating her on the bed and exiting just as Al arrived. All I could hope was that I'd planted enough reasonable doubt to avoid conviction in Carol's ever-suspicious mind.

CHAPTER 15

BEING SUMMER PEOPLE

We all slept in on Sunday. I was the first one up because I was awakened at 9:30 by the pressure of a cool feline nose against mine. Sherlock Holmes had waited long enough for his homecoming breakfast.

After filling Sherlock's dish, I made a pot of coffee and went back upstairs to shower, shave and put on a powder blue polo shirt, navy blue shorts and a new pair of black flip-flops I'd purchased in one of the many tourist traps on Circuit Avenue. The darn things kept sliding off my feet as I went down the stairs and I decided that I'd have to change to more secure footwear before going beyond the porch.

When I went into to the kitchen for coffee, Carol was heading toward the porch with a full mug in her hand. She was wrapped in a pale blue bathrobe, her always-perfect hair was splayed like a sunburst and her feet were bare.

"I was afraid I'd drown if I didn't have a jolt of caffeine before getting in the shower," she said as I settled into a chair beside her.

"Harry's party wear you out?" I asked.

"It did. But not as much as Harry's girlfriend must have worn you out."

"A, she is not Harry's girlfriend because Harry prefers boys and, B, escorting her to her room wasn't all that exhausting, even if she did lean on me pretty heavily for support." When I said support, I meant physical, not moral.

"You're sticking with that story, are you?"

"I always stick with the truth. That's why I'm an award-winning reporter."

"If you say so," Carol said. She didn't sound convinced.

I was searching for a way to dispel her doubt when Dave Jerome shuffled onto the porch, dressed for the day in a hot yellow T-shirt, red shorts and sandals. He mumbled a greeting and sat down with his coffee. Carol finished hers, said it was time for a shower and went upstairs.

Dave and I sat in silence for several minutes, sipping coffee and watching a parade of puffy white clouds drift across the sky. Another day of blue skies and sunshine was beginning.

"So," he said at last. "Did you get in a quicky with the cute blond chicky before Al found you last night?"

"The chicky, as you so callously refer to the lovely lady from Lindstrom, went off to dreamland a minute after I helped her into the room," I said. "She'd downed enough gin and wine to put a horse in a coma."

"Too bad. She's got a hell of a body and she looked like she was desperate to share it with you."

"Let's not go there anymore, okay? I'd just as soon give Carol time to forget about Rhonda before Martha comes home in November."

Dave nodded and we finished our coffee in silence. One by one, the others joined us and we went off to Linda Jean's for brunch, which required a 20-minute wait outside. When at last we got a table, we discussed our options and decided to make this an actual vacation day. We would tour Martha's Vineyard in our genuine island car without worrying about the whereabouts of Uncle

Walt, the key to the treasure map code or the villainy of the man who had stolen Sherlock Holmes.

Before we took off, I had some calls to make. I actually caught Martha at home and I gave her a selective report on Harry Dick's party. I described the facility, the food and the festivities, but I saw no need to mention the gallant escort service I had provided for Ms. Fairchild.

The next call went to my mother and grandmother at the farm in Harmony. I discovered that I'd forgotten to send a birthday card to Grandma Goodie the previous week and my mother poured on a full measure of guilt. This was followed by the usual pitch for the salvation of my soul by Grandma Goodie, who was more concerned about my failing to attend church than my birthday card faux pas.

"Warnie baby," Grandma Goodie said when my mother passed the phone to her. "Did you go to church this morning?"

"This is an island filled with summer people looking for rest and relaxation," I said. "All the churches are on vacation."

"I don't believe that for a minute," she said. "The Lord never takes a vacation, summer or otherwise."

"Well, there's a plaque in this cottage that says God created Nantucket but He lives on Martha's Vineyard, so maybe I'll find Him on the beach."

"Don't you be joking about your soul, Warnie baby. God could take you at any time and you should be prepared."

"You're right," I said, recalling how close God had come to taking me on my previous visit to the Vineyard. "I'll do my best to get to church next Sunday." I knew my best wouldn't be good enough, especially since we'd be spending all day boating, busing, flying and cabbing to get home, but it sounded conciliatory and we ended the conversation with our usual expressions of love.

Since we would-be vacationers had seen quite a bit of Edgartown and Chappaquiddick, we decided to go up-island. Checking the map, we found a way to avoid the traffic tangle in Vineyard Haven on our way to West Tisbury. We browsed through two art galleries there, indulged ourselves at a popular—and expensive—chocolate shop in Chilmark, checked out the commercial fishing fleet in the harbor at Menemsha and climbed a hill to view the multi-colored Gay Head cliffs in the little town of Aquinnah.

At the cliffs, parking was so limited that we had to loop around a large open field of grass and drive through the designated area three times before a spot opened up. As we circled, Al observed that the black Chevy sedan behind us on all three passes was the same car that had parked behind us at the two art galleries and within sight of us at both the chocolate shop and Menemsha harbor. We were being followed again.

"Wonder if it's the same crew that followed us before," Dave said.

"Let's stay here for a few minutes and see if they come around again," I said. "We can get their license number and ask our favorite detective to check it out again."

We stood around the car pretending to have a casual conversation, but the black Chevy didn't appear. After a few minutes, we said the hell with it and walked up the steep path to look at the cliffs, the lighthouse and the ocean. Cindy pointed out that some of the people on the beach far below us seemed to be wearing flesh-colored swimsuits. A look through Dave's binoculars at a sun-tanned woman displaying what had appeared to be a pink bikini reminded us that we'd read about Gayhead being another clothing-optional beach.

"Hope she's got plenty of sun block on those tender areas," Dave said.

Cindy took the binoculars, checked out one of the men and

remarked that he should have chosen the other option.

On the way down from the observation point, we wandered through a couple of shops. In one, we found items actually made by Martha's Vineyard Wampanoag tribe members. In the other, many of the *Native American* souvenirs were marked "Made in China." We bought some over-priced ice cream cones and were only a few steps from the parking lot when the Chevy cruised by. As always, Al's camera was around his neck and he grabbed a quick, one-handed shot of the retreating vehicle. We had the number on the license plate.

★ ★ ★

My first phone call Monday morning was to Detective Gouveia.

"For God's sake, you guys from Minnesota are more trouble than all the rest of the summer people combined," Manny said. "Why the hell is somebody following you now?"

"Who knows?" I said. My suspicion was that they were hoping we'd lead them to Walt Jerome, but I kept this to myself.

Manny called back an hour later, saying the car was another rental and that the renter again was Dirk Oberman, owner of the Bottoms Up.

"I think it's time for us to drive to Vineyard Haven and have a chat with Mr. Oberman," I said.

"Not necessary," Manny said. "They've moved their tub to Oak Bluffs. They're tied up close enough to the All That Glitters to hear a guy fart on the poop deck."

"Do you think they're sneaking aboard the All That Glitters looking for the treasure map?"

"We've got a hundred feet of crime scene tape and an armed officer that says they're not."

"You've got an armed officer onboard?"

"Damn straight. He'll be there until we find a security agency to watch the boat 24/seven."

"Have you found the chart that Morgan took from me when he whacked me on the head?" I asked.

"Not yet," Manny said. "And Morgan ain't talkin' to us. He lawyered-up with his first phone call and hasn't said a word to us since. Which reminds me, where did you guys get that chart?"

Oh, oh! I couldn't tell him we'd got it from the missing Walt Jerome. "We found it," I said. "It was hidden outside the cottage."

"Oh, yeah? Where?"

I had to think fast. "It was, uh, in the garbage can," I said, recalling our search for the wastebasket copy. "We found it taped to the side when we put out a bag of trash."

"Really?" he said in a tone that meant "bullshit."

"Yes, really. It was out there while you guys were inside tearing the cottage apart."

"If you say so." He sounded as disbelieving as Carol when I told her I hadn't been in the sack with Rhonda Fairchild. "Must have smelled really good."

"Oh, yeah," I said. "I'm surprised you haven't sniffed it out on the All That Glitters."

"We'll take my dog along next time we search. And you guys watch your ass if you go and talk to the Bottoms Up crew. Like I said, they ain't a very friendly-lookin' bunch."

"Should we carry our paintball guns?"

"You do and you'll be decoratin' a jail cell. Put them things into that trash can and send 'em to the dump. Have a good day, Mr. Mitchell."

A good day? Visiting the boys on the Bottoms Up didn't sound like a very good way to start it, but I relayed the news about the boat's new docking place to Al and Dave and away we went to the harbor. Cindy and Carol said they were going to the town beach to catch some morning rays and would meet us back at the cottage in time for lunch.

Manny hadn't been kidding about the minuscule distance between the two treasure hunter boats. The Bottoms Up was tied up directly behind the All That Glitters, so close that you could jump from the bow of the former to the stern of the latter. The primary impediment to such a leap was a band of yellow crime scene tape that encircled the All That Glitters. A secondary impediment was a uniformed police officer perched in the chair formerly occupied by Charles Morgan. As Manny had suggested, if this officer passed gas at even a modest decibel level, the sound would be heard aboard the Bottoms Up.

We waved at the officer as we passed the All That Glitters and stopped beside the Bottoms Up. It appeared to be deserted, but Dave called out for Captain Oberman and a head appeared in a hatch from below deck near the stern. The head was gleaming bald, featured a Z-shaped scar from the right cheek bone to the bewhiskered jaw and bore multiple silver adornments that were plugged into a variety of perforations. Smoke curled from the stub of a cigarette that dangled from a fat pair of lips and two beady dark eyes peered from under bushy, black brows. It was, as the saying goes, not a pretty sight.

"Who wants the captain?" asked the head.

"The people he's been following all around the island," Dave said.

"Well, people, you're out of luck," the head said. The body underneath the head climbed higher on the ladder, stopping with its expansive belly at deck level. The shirtless shoulders and chest were covered with a shag rug of black hair that extended all the way down to the navel. "The captain's gone ashore."

"When do you expect him back, Mister…?" Dave asked.

"Don't rightly know," he said. "And it's Mr. Shaughnessy here. Who might you be?"

"I'm David Jerome, and for some reason I seem to be of interest to your captain. You can tell him I stopped by and that I'll be back this evening."

Shaughnessy hauled his belly, which I estimated at a good 48 inches in circumference, through the hatch and climbed onto the deck. I was relieved to see that beneath his belly he was wearing a grease-splotched pair of khaki trousers. "I'm sure the captain will be thrilled," he said.

"Me, too," Dave said. "Have a nice day." Shaughnessy's response was to toss the cigarette butt over the side into the narrow strip of water between the boat and the dock.

We walked back to our cottage and found a man sitting and rocking on the porch. He rose to greet us and I was impressed with his resemblance to a Sumo wrestler. He stood at least six-foot-three and had to weigh in the neighborhood of 300 pounds, which is a neighborhood I'd rather not visit. His shoulder-length black hair hung straight around his head, almost hiding the two-inch gold loops that dangled from his ears. I guessed his age at about 35.

"Welcome back, gentlemen," the man said. "I'm Dirk Oberman."

CHAPTER 16

SPECIAL CIRCUMSTANCES

Dave offered Oberman a drink—beer, pop, water, what have you. The big man declined and we sat in a semi-circle regarding each other in silence until Dave asked the obvious question. "Why have you been following us?"

"Why do you think?" Oberman replied.

"I asked you first," Dave said.

Oberman's lips formed a thin smile. "It shouldn't be that hard to figure out. I want to talk to Walter Jerome, and I think you know where he is."

"I did," said Dave. "But I don't anymore so you might as well save your gas. Why do you want to talk to him anyway?"

"I think he's got something I want."

"Which is?"

"Wade Waters's chart. I know that Waters found the wreck and marked it on a chart. We asked his buddy, Morgan, about the chart and he said Waters gave it to the guy who wrote the magazine article. That would be Walter Jerome."

"Did it occur to you that Morgan might be lying?" Dave asked. "That he might have the chart?"

"We questioned him under special circumstances that made it unproductive for him to lie," Oberman said. Again he smiled, but there was no humor in it.

"I hope you're not planning to question any of us under those special circumstances," Al said.

"I came here hoping that it wouldn't be necessary," Oberman said. "I was hoping you'd give me a steer to Walter Jerome."

"Well, Mr. Oberman, I can't do that, and I wouldn't do it if I could," Dave said. "And I'm curious about what you know about Wade Waters' death."

"All I know is what I read in the papers," Oberman said. "Waters went out alone because Morgan went ashore to meet an old friend, the boat was found drifting without nobody on it several hours later, and a lucky fisherman snagged the body in the sound a week after that."

"You're sure you and your crew didn't question Waters under your special brand of circumstances?" I asked.

"We all have alibis for that day," Oberman said. "Morgan hasn't been able to prove that his is real." I remembered Manny saying that to Morgan, but I also couldn't help wondering how real Oberman and company's alibis were.

"It's been nice chatting with you, Mr. Oberman," Dave said as he rose from his chair. "Sorry we couldn't help you."

"That's the way it goes," Oberman said, rising and towering over Dave. "Maybe you'll be able to help me later."

"Like I said, I wouldn't if I could," Dave said.

"Sometimes a person doesn't get a choice," Oberman said. With another humorless smile, he nodded, said, "Good day, gentlemen," and walked down the steps and away.

"Judging from those two creeps, Manny wasn't kidding about that crew," Al said when Oberman was out of earshot.

"We don't go anywhere alone and we always watch for them to be following us," Dave said. "I sure as hell don't want to be questioned under Oberman's special kind of circumstances. I wonder if Wade Waters was."

The wives returned and we grilled some hotdogs for lunch. When we finished, I called the *Gazette* and asked for Terry Shaw. She was out on an assignment, so I left a message.

We spent the rest of the day doing actual vacation stuff. The women wanted to check out some shops and we men surprised them by tagging along. Because of our conversation with Dirk Oberman, we didn't want Carol and Cindy wandering around by themselves anymore, but we didn't tell them that.

★ ★ ★

Terry Shaw returned my call while I was drinking coffee on the porch after breakfast Tuesday. She sounded a bit apprehensive when I told her I was a reporter and wanted to talk about Wade Waters, but her resistance melted when I told her who I had come to the Vineyard with and whose cottage I was staying in.

"Do you guys know where Walt is?" Terry asked.

"No," I said. "We found him last week, but he's disappeared again."

"We're all worried sick about him," she said. "He's still got a lot of friends here at the paper, you know. We've been wondering if the guy who killed Wade Waters got him, too."

"Walt was extremely alive and well last week. We're guessing that he's still in that condition, but he seems to be hiding from both the killer and the cops."

Terry said she'd love to meet Walt's nephew and suggested that he and I join her for lunch at 12:30 in a restaurant on the waterfront in Edgartown. This was the response I was hoping for.

Dave and I took off for Edgartown in the rust bucket at a few minutes after noon. Al said he would "hang out with the girls" until we got back. All the way to Edgartown, I kept watching to see if we had a following, but we seemed to be free of the Bottoms Up boys.

We'd forgotten about the hopeless parking situation in Edgartown and we almost got lost winding through the streets looking for an open spot. It took so long to find one eight blocks from the restaurant that we had to walk all the way at top speed to arrive only five minutes late.

"How will we know this woman?" Dave asked as we reached the front door. "Did you get a description?"

"She said to ask the hostess," I said. "Apparently she eats there enough to be known."

The temperature, in the 80s, was matched by the relative humidity, so we were both mopping sweat off our faces when we asked the hostess to seat us with Terry Shaw. The prim, perfectly-coiffed redhead, who'd been basking in air conditioning all day, wrinkled her dainty nose, told us to follow her and led us to a table in the back corner.

Terry rose to greet us. She was one of those wiry, athletic people who could be any age from 50 to 75. Her skin, which had been exposed to thousands of hours in the Vineyard sun, was tanned and wrinkled and looked like 75. The hand she offered for shaking was smooth and strong, more in line with 50. Her short, straight hair was snowy white, possibly another product of the sun, and I guessed her actual age to be somewhere between 60 and 65.

It was obvious that Terry was much more interested in Dave than she was in me. She expressed her concern for his missing uncle, told him how much Walt was loved and respected by everyone who knew him, and wished Dave luck in finding him again. Finally, she turned to me and asked what I hoped to learn from her.

I told her about our adventures with Charles Morgan and

said I'd like to get more background on the late Wade Waters. "In addition to my natural reporter's curiosity about any murder case, this one has gotten personal," I said.

"Didn't you read Walt's story in the magazine?" Terry asked.

"I did, but it was mostly about his work salvaging treasure and the current hunt for the wreck of the Daniel French. I'd like to know more about Wade Waters' life on the Vineyard before he took up treasure hunting. Your photographer, a guy named Streeter, told me you've been covering that scene for, uh, quite a number of years."

"Did he tell you that I was here when Captain Gosnold landed in the 1600s?" she asked.

"Not in so many words," I said.

"I'm surprised. He usually tells people that I've been here longer than the Wampanoags. Actually, I am closing in on 40 years of covering everything that happens on the waters around the Vineyard."

A pretty young woman wearing a white, scoop-neck blouse and crisply-creased khaki shorts arrived at our table. She brushed a loose lock of dark hair away from her eyes and announced that her name was Bambi and she would be our server. We all ordered iced tea and said we needed a few minutes to look at the menu. As Bambi walked away, I noticed that the shorts fit snugly around a tiny waist and two nicely rounded cheeks.

"How far back do you want to go on Wade Waters?" Terry asked while we perused the luncheon selections.

"As far back as you know," I said. "Cradle to grave if possible."

"Afraid I can't do cradle. He was born off-island and I think he was close to teen-age when his parents moved here."

"Are the parents still on the island?"

"No, they moved to Florida when Wayne's dad retired. Massachusetts people do that, you know."

"Wayne's dad? Who's Wayne?"

"Wayne is Wade's real name. He changed it when he went into hunting for sunken treasure because Wade Waters was more colorful." I was glad to learn that the Waters family hadn't really named their son Wade.

"Any brothers or sisters?" I asked.

"One sister," Terry said. "She's married and living in the Midwest somewhere. I think it's one of the M-states—Michigan or Minnesota or Montana. They all run together for me."

Before I could enlighten her on the differences, Bambi returned with our iced tea, brushed the unruly lock away from her eyes and asked if we were ready to order. Terry ordered fried clams, the complete kind with bellies. Although she recommended them, we midland Americans weren't quite up to eating clam bellies so we both ordered fish and chips.

"Okay," I said as I watched Bambi depart. "So back when Wade was called Wayne, what did he do?"

"Well, in high school he was a hockey hotshot, and the girls thought he was quite a hunk," Terry said. "I remember our sports writer commenting on how many groupies were waiting for him outside the locker room after every game."

"Did he go to college?"

"He got a hockey scholarship at Clarkson, but he only lasted a year. He was more interested in chasing pucks and pussy than he was in passing tests so he finished the year on probation and wouldn't have been eligible to play hockey the next semester."

"Did he come back home?"

"Yes. He came back and picked up jobs crewing on some of the tourist boats. That's how he wound up working with Henry Agnew."

"Whoa!" I said. "Did you say he worked with Henry Agnew?"

"Yes. He started out crewing on Henry's catamarans and they eventually became partners in the business."

"I talked to Henry Agnew at a party Saturday night and he told me he had met Wade Waters 'sometime or other,' but didn't really know him."

"Why would he tell you that?" Terry asked.

"My question exactly. I think I'll ask him."

"You must have misunderstood Henry. They worked together for several years until Wayne decided to go hunting for shipwrecks and took off for Florida about 10 years ago. Come to think of it, it was 10 years exactly. I remember it because he got out just ahead of a major nor'easter that wrecked a couple of fishing boats based at Menemsha."

"Did he just take off all by himself?"

"Not quite all by himself. There was a woman with him—one of the dollies he met on the catamaran, I think. I remember that her last name was Smith because that's such a common name. Her first name was something like Carol or Kayla, but I'm not sure exactly."

"How did Agnew react to his partner's leaving?"

"Didn't seem to bother him much. He stayed cool like he always was, took over running the whole cat and sailboat operation like he had at the start and hired an accountant to do his bookwork."

"What happened to the woman, do you know?" I asked.

"I don't know," she said. "There was no woman with Wade this spring when he brought his boat into Oak Bluffs. Just that creepy Morgan character."

"Walt's story said Charles Morgan was a new crew member—that he'd left a previous partner in Florida."

"That would be Buck Studwell. They were classmates in high school. Played hockey together. Buck went to Florida to join

Wayne, or Wade, a couple years after Wade left the Vineyard."

"Seems like Wade had a thing for walking away from partners."

"He wasn't noted for either his loyalty or his diplomacy," Terry said. "I heard from several people who worked for him here in Edgartown that he was an arrogant son of a bitch."

Bambi arrived with our food and set the plates on the table. She brushed the hair away from her eyes and asked if there was anything else she could do for us. I wanted to suggest pulling her hair back into a ponytail so she could see what she was serving, but I held my tongue and enjoyed the view again as she retreated. I noted that the vertical creases in her shorts perfectly bisected the oval outlines of her glutei maximi. A good reporter looks for such details.

"Better check your French fries for long, dark strands of hair," Dave said as he examined his.

"Some of these college girls are hard to train," Terry said. "Summer service can be an adventure but the food here is always good."

She was right. The fish and chips were excellent, and I left Bambi a generous tip, hoping she would use it to buy a hair clip.

Dave drove us back to Oak Bluffs and I forgot about watching for a tail while we soaked in the beauty of the flawless blue canopy above us and the multi-colored layers of seawater glistening beyond the bright umbrellas studding the sandy beach. When we pulled up in front of Walt's cottage, another male stranger was making himself at home on the porch. We were drawing as much traffic as a Greyhound bus station.

CHAPTER 17

FRIENDSHIP

Our newest visitor was short and muscular, with crew-cut blond hair and a square face. His red muscle shirt emphasized the strength of his shoulders and his navy blue shorts revealed muscular, hairy legs. He was clean-shaven and wore no skin-piercing adornments in his ears or on his face. He didn't get up when Dave and I climbed the steps to the porch.

"Can we help you?" Dave asked in an unhelpful tone.

"Maybe you can and maybe you can't," the man said. "My name is Buck Studwell and I used to work with Wade Waters."

"I've heard of you," Dave said. "What do you think we maybe can do for you?"

"Word around the island is that you guys have a chart that belonged to Wade Waters—a chart that shows where the wreck of the Daniel French lies."

"Word around the island is a little behind times," I said. "We did have a chart, but a guy named Morgan, who you might know, took it away from us."

"So I've heard," Studwell said. "What I'm betting on is that you made a copy and kept it."

"You lose your bet," Dave said.

"Oh, please," Studwell said. "I wasn't born yesterday and neither were you. You copied that chart and that copy is rightfully mine."

"How do you figure that?" I asked.

"I was Wade's partner before he took on this Morgan freak and he never bought back my share of the boat. Obviously, Morgan is going to jail for killing Wade, which leaves me as the owner of the boat and the chart. I'm willing to pay a finder's fee for the chart, so name your price."

"How do we know you didn't kill Waters?" I asked. "Quite a coincidence, you showing up here right when he died."

"I read a story in the Miami paper that said Wade was missing. I was afraid the worst had happened, so I flew up here to help look for him, but by the time I got here, his body had been found."

"You didn't come until after the body was found?" Dave asked.

"That's right. I can show you my airline boarding pass if you don't believe me."

"You could also have made a roundtrip that you won't show us the boarding passes for, several days before the body was found," I said.

"You guys are way too suspicious," Studwell said. "There's no way you can say that I'm the killer."

"You just gave us a motive when you claimed to be the heir to everything the dead man owned," I said.

"Oh, come on, let's cut the bullshit and talk about a deal," Studwell said. "You name your price and I tell you how much I'll add to it when I haul up the treasure from the Daniel French."

"Sorry," Dave said. "We don't have the location of the wreck and we wouldn't sell it if we did."

Studwell stood up. "You're making a big mistake, gentlemen. When the crew from the Bottoms Up comes calling, you'll wish you'd taken the money from me and run back to the mainland."

"You know the Bottoms Up crew, do you?" Dave asked.

"Not any more than I have to," Studwell said. "They're a nasty bunch when they're racing you to find a wreck."

"How come you're not still Wade Waters' partner?" I asked.

"I quit when Carly died," he said.

"Who's Carly?" Dave asked.

"Carly Smith," Studwell said. "Wade's girlfriend. Or what do they call it now? Significant other?"

"Is Carly the woman who went to Florida with him when he bailed out on Henry Agnew?" I asked.

"You're pretty smart for an off-islander," Studwell said. "Yeah, Carly went along to Florida, and it cost her her life."

"How so?" I asked.

"She died in a diving accident," he said. "She was crewing with Wade and me, but one morning the two of them went out without me to the site of a wreck we'd been working. I don't know if they were planning to spend the whole day screwing on the deck in the sunshine or what, but late in the afternoon she went into the water without a backup diver and her gear got tangled in the wreck. By the time Wade figured out she was in trouble and got into his gear and got down to her, Carly was dead. It tore him up something awful. I think Carly was the only thing besides money that Wade ever loved."

"And you consoled your friend by quitting on him?" Dave said.

"I couldn't work for that operation anymore," Studwell said. "To tell you the truth, I was in love with Carly as much as he was, but I never tried to do anything about it."

"Well, I'm sorry we can't help you find the Daniel French," Dave said. "Anyway, the coordinates were written in code, and the code went to heaven with your former partner."

"I'll bet I could break the code," Studwell said. "Wade wasn't a rocket scientist, you know."

"Bye now," Dave said.

Studwell shrugged, went down the porch steps and turned back to face us. "I'll stay in touch in case you find another copy," he said. "And you guys stay ready to hear from the Bottoms Up crew. Adios, amigos."

"How do you like that?" Dave said. "He didn't even say goodbye."

We sat down to await the return of the rest of the Vineyard vacationers. I was wondering how many more large, ill-tempered men would come looking for the treasure map when my cell phone sounded off. It was a small, ill-tempered man, City Editor Don O'Rourke, asking why I hadn't sent any new stories about the missing Walter Jerome.

"There's nothing new to report," I said. "Our former editor is still missing and the cops still have no clue. They did arrest the man who stole my cat and they seem to think that he killed the man Walt wrote his last big story about. That man is still dead, by the way."

"I'm happy for your cat and sorry for the dead man," Don said. "Now put together something for tomorrow morning. What are we paying you for?"

"Right now you're supposed to be paying me for two weeks' vacation."

"Don't be a smartass. You know reporters are never really on vacation. Not good reporters, anyway."

"Since you put it that way, you'll have 24 inches of copy, including background details of Walt's 15 years as editor of the *Daily Dispatch*, from me before deadline."

"How about six inches," Don said. "Good reporters also write tight."

"Now what?" Dave asked when I snapped my phone shut.

"Don's worried about your uncle," I said.

"So am I. Where the hell can he be hiding?"

"Should we go look on Chappy to see if he's come back?"

"That might be tomorrow's project. Or we could stake out the grocery store and see if Daffy Dolly will lead us to him again."

"You can follow her on the bike this time," I said. "My legs have barely stopped hurting from last week's chase."

"Maybe she'd tell you where he is if you asked her," Dave said. "She knows that Uncle Walt talked to you."

"Yeah, after he threatened to put a load of buckshot up my butt."

"But your butt is still buckshot free."

"Whatever. Finding Daffy Dolly is a shot in the dark, and I don't feel like standing around in the heat all day targeting somebody who might never show up."

"Yeah, I don't blame you. This was supposed to be an unforgettable vacation for you. But we need to do something pretty soon. We've only got four days left on this island." We had tickets for an afternoon flight home from Boston on Sunday, which meant we'd be leaving the Vineyard on an early ferry and catching a bus to Logan International Airport.

"Well, if you think of something other than staking out the grocery store let me know," I said. "Meanwhile, I have a story to write."

I went up to my room and opened my laptop. Before beginning to write, I checked my e-mail and found nothing from Martha. I decided to call her and punched in the number, but she didn't answer. Neither did her machine.

"Now what the hell?" I said out loud. Sherlock Holmes, who was stretched out beside my pillow, opened his eyes, flicked his ears and went back to sleep. I apologized for disturbing him and started tapping out my story.

* * *

Vacation or no vacation, we decided to be proactive on all fronts Wednesday morning. Dave and Cindy drove to Chappy to check out Walt's former hiding place. Al, Carol and I, carrying cell phones, staked out the area all around the Reliable Market. Al and Carol watched the front door facing Circuit Avenue and I patrolled the parking lot in the rear. The plan was that if Al or Carol saw Daffy Dolly they would summon me to question her, which I would do while blocking her path to the bike. No more pedaling pursuits for me.

The sun beat down from a cloudless sky as the temperature again rose toward the 80s. After cooking for a couple of hours, I phoned Al and suggested trading places. He came to the parking lot and I went to join Carol on the shady side of the building.

At a few minutes before noon, all five of us met for a pre-arranged muster at Linda Jean's. None of us had anything positive to report.

"Those assholes from the Bottoms Up tailed us, but we lost them by going through the triangle parking lot and squeezing into the traffic several cars ahead of them," Dave said. "We did some extra zigzagging through Edgartown before we went to the On Time ferry and never saw them again."

"All we got for our morning's work was another layer of sunburn," Al said. "My skin is as red as diaper rash on a baby's ass."

"Maybe you need some Oil of Olay," I said.

"That's a bully suggestion," he said. "Now please picador and leave."

"You'll find me on the Cape," I said, pointing toward the mainland.

As we rose and moved toward the door, I almost collided with Detective Gouveia. "Hey," he said. "What are you guys doin' here?"

"Just hanging out, doing our thing," I said. "Where should we be?"

"In court," Manny said. "Your pal Morgan is comin' in for arraignment at two o'clock. All the TV guys from Boston and Providence are already there."

"Damn it!" I said. "Nobody told us. What's the charge?"

"Murder one. His alibi about stayin' on the island to meet an old friend while Waters went out alone doesn't check out. Number one, he can't produce the old friend. And, number two, we put him in a lineup and the bartender and the waitress he claims he ordered from told us they'd never seen him before."

"Wasn't the All That Glitters found abandoned in Nantucket Sound?" Al asked. "How'd Morgan get back to the island after whacking his partner?"

"That's the one piece we're missin'," Manny said. "We think he had a small boat, maybe an inflatable, hid on board or tied behind the All That Glitters. We're lookin' hard for that boat and when we find it, we'll have Morgan right by the…well, you know." He'd noticed in mid-sentence that Carol and Cindy were listening intently.

"Where's the courthouse?" Dave asked.

"Main Street of Edgartown," Manny said. "Right next to the Old Whalin' Church."

We left the detective to eat his lunch in peace and hurried back to the car that Dave had left parked at Walt's cottage. We stuffed ourselves in and drove to Edgartown. We'd seen the Old Whaling Church, a huge white frame building with massive white columns on the front, so we found the courthouse with no problem. What we didn't find without a problem was a parking place anywhere near the building. After circling several blocks, Cindy and Carol volunteered to continue the search while Dave, Al and I ran to the courthouse.

It was only a minute before 2 when we dashed into the courtroom, which contained more reporters and TV cameras than regular spectators. Dripping sweat and not wishing to submit any innocent strangers to our body odors, we stood in the back of the room. As always, Al was carrying his camera and he took some shots of the crowd while we waited for the judge to appear.

The Honorable Harold O'Connor, a dried-up, gray-haired man with hearing aids and extremely thick glasses, strode in at 2:01. After the required ceremony of all who were seated rising and being seated again, the case of the Commonwealth of Massachusetts versus Charles Morgan was called.

Morgan, wearing an orange jumpsuit and a set of shiny handcuffs, was brought in by two state troopers. A thirtyish man dressed in a dark business suit stepped up beside Morgan and introduced himself to the court as "Lester Byrd with a Y" from the public defender's office.

County Attorney Elizabeth Winthrop, conservatively attired in the same navy blue pants suit she'd worn at the press conference, read the charge of murder in the first degree. She stated a list of facts pointing toward Morgan's guilt, including the discovery of the murder victim's chart—the one so rudely snatched away from me—among Morgan's personal belongings.

"How do you plead?" Judge O'Connor asked, leaning forward, squinting through his heavy lenses and cocking his head to hear better.

"Not guilty," Morgan said in a voice loud enough to be heard on the street.

Still leaning forward, straining to see and hear the attorneys before him, the octogenarian judge set a preliminary hearing for

October and discussed the question of bail with both sides before denying it. Judge O'Connor's head was almost hanging over the edge of the bench by the time he ordered Morgan back to jail and rapped his gavel to end the proceeding. As soon as everyone turned away from the bench, the judge sat back, closed his eyes and wiped his brow with the sleeve of his black robe. This had been a real workout for a man accustomed to hearing cases involving minor misdemeanors and traffic transgressions.

As we were leaving the courtroom, Cindy and Carol were coming up the steps. We watched the media mob straggle out, Al shot a few more pictures out of habit and the women led us to the car, which was parked four blocks away.

On the way back, Dave wondered aloud about finding his uncle and giving him the news. "Now that Morgan's charged with the murder and sitting behind bars, Uncle Walt's got nothing to worry about," Dave said.

"That's not completely true," Al said. "There are still some very unpleasant people looking for the chart that Waters gave your uncle."

We found one of those unpleasant people sitting on the porch when we reached the cottage. I made a mental note to start taking in the chairs every time we went away.

CHAPTER 18

WHAT PRICE SAFETY?

Our current unpleasant visitor was Dirk Oberman, the 300-pound head nasty of the Bottoms Up. He rose to greet us, which allowed him to tower over and around 5-foot-10, 170-pound Dave Jerome.

"To what do we owe this pleasure?" Dave asked. Neither man put out a hand for shaking.

"Got a deal for you," Oberman said. "I'm tired of playing games."

"Me, too," Dave said. "What have you got in mind?"

We all sat down, with Dave and Oberman in the middle and two of us on each side. Dave was on Oberman's right and I drew the chair on his left.

"I'm willing to pay you a very substantial amount of cash for your copy of Wade Waters's chart," Oberman said. "In addition, I'll cut you in on a percentage of what we find in the wreck."

"What if I don't have a copy of the chart?" Dave asked.

"Cut the bullshit," Oberman said. "I know you gave the chart to Morgan. The DA said in court this afternoon that the cops found it in his stuff. You'd be a fucking idiot—pardon my French, ladies—not to have made a copy."

Dave looked at Cindy, who was pretending to be perturbed by

the F-word, before he replied. "How much cash and what percentage are you offering?"

"Ten thousand cash and 5 percent of the profits," Oberman said.

"Peanuts," Dave said.

"Chicken feed," I said.

"Bread crumbs," Al said.

Oberman scowled. "Okay, make it 20,000 and 10 percent."

"You're insulting our intelligence," Dave said.

"We weren't born yesterday," I said.

"We're not fucking idiots," Al said. Cindy put her fingertips to her lips as though offended again, while Carol coughed and hid a smile behind her hand.

"All right," Oberman said. "How much *do* you people want?"

"Fifty grand and 50 percent," Dave said.

"Are you shittin' me?" Oberman said.

"Not a bit," Dave said.

"Perfect fit," I said.

"No shit," Al said.

Oberman stared at our expressionless faces for a full minute. "Twenty-five thou and 15 percent," he said. "That's tops. Take it or leave it."

"We'll leave it for the time being," Dave said. "We have another bidder who might top your tops."

"What do you mean another bidder? This ain't no fucking auction." Cindy put an index finger into each of her ears and Oberman said, "Oh, sorry."

Carol was still covering her mouth and I was afraid she might explode.

"What I mean is that we have another person who is interested in the chart," Dave said. "We'll run your offer by him and see if he'll go higher."

"If you're talking about that loser Studwell, forget it," Oberman said. "He ain't got that kind of money up front and he's too tight to give you any kind of a percentage."

"Maybe we'd be better off keeping the chart and hiring a diving crew," Dave said. "If we had a chart, that is."

Oberman rose and Dave stood up to face him. Oberman's tone was ominous. "If you do that, you'd better also buy some damn good life insurance." He went down the steps and turned to face us. "You talk to your other bidder and see what he offers. I'll be back tomorrow to see how you made out." He turned away and rumbled off toward the harbor.

Cindy grabbed Dave's arm and spun him toward her. "Would you really do that?"

"Do what?" he asked.

"Hire divers and go looking for the wreck."

"No, I don't think so. But Uncle Walt might if we could find him and he could break the code."

"Studwell thinks he can break the code," Al said. "Plus he's probably got a legal right to the All That Glitters. Maybe we should team up with him."

"He left us his cell phone number," I said.

"I don't know what the hell to do," Dave said. "I'd give my right arm to find Uncle Walt right now."

"That's your drawing arm," Cindy said. "Give away something less valuable."

"Your right brain maybe," I said.

"Or your right nut," Al said.

"Oh, no!" Cindy gasped. "Not that!" She pretended to swoon and we all had a much-needed laugh.

We decided to salvage what was left of the afternoon by going to State Beach. Before changing into my swimming trunks, I checked my e-mail. Nothing from Martha Todd. Two straight days without an e-mail or a phone call. Calculating that it was a few minutes past 7 in Cape Verde, I punched in her phone number. Again no answer and no answering machine. What the hell was going on out there?

★ ★ ★

After a leisurely supper of swordfish, grilled superbly by Al, and the trimmings, prepared skillfully by Carol and Cindy, Dave suggested going to the 9 p.m. movie in the theater at the foot of Circuit Avenue. It was a mediocre pirate film that I'd seen the night before we left St. Paul, so I opted to say at the cottage and fiddle with a freelance piece I'd started about the perils of a Martha's Vineyard vacation. With luck, I'd sell it to a magazine for enough money to pay for the plane ticket.

I was pecking away on my laptop at the dining room table when the kitchen phone rang. Should I answer it? Was it another hard case looking for Wade Waters' treasure map? Was it the Oak Bluffs police with news about Walt Jerome? Or could it be Walt himself, wondering if it was safe to come home? I decided to pick it up.

"Is Mitch there?" asked a female voice.

"This is Mitch," I said. "Who are you?"

"It's me, silly. Rhonda Fairchild."

Oh, God, I thought. "Oh, hi," I said.

"I'm really glad you're there," Rhonda said. "I need your help."

"What kind of help?"

"I need a place to stay tonight."

"Why? You've got a beautiful room at the Sweet Whatever It Is."

"Not anymore," she said. "Harry kicked me out of Summer Sweet."

"Why would he do that?" I asked.

"He wanted me to screw a fat, ugly friend of his who swings both ways. In the daylight, yet. I said, 'no way am I doing that,' and Harry said, 'no way am I keeping you in this expensive room.' It was like being back in high school where the guys told you to either put out or walk home."

I wanted to ask which option she'd selected in high school. Instead, I asked her where she was calling from.

"I'm in Oak Bluffs, which is where you said you were staying. I took a taxi from Summer Sweet and the driver let me off at a little square with benches and trees on a street he called Circuit Avenue. He said anybody, even an off-islander, could find me here."

Unfortunately, the driver was right. Even I could find her. She was at David M. Healey Square, across the street from our favorite restaurant. The question was, should I tell her I knew where she was or should I play dumb and say she'd better find a hotel room?

Being soft of both heart and head, I advised her to sit down on one of those benches and wait for me. She thanked me and said she'd make it worth my while. Oh, sure she would, with Al and Carol occupying the room right across the hall from mine.

Rhonda greeted me with a hug and a kiss that involved almost enough tongue to clean my tonsils. Her boobs were encased in an overstretched white tube top and her buns were barely covered by a pair of form-fitting white shorts. Even under the artificial light from the street lamps, the contrast between her clothing and her suntanned skin was striking. After we broke the clinch and stepped apart, I saw several guys turn their heads for a lingering look as they walked by.

Rhonda had two large bags, a carry-on bag and a monstrous purse. Fortunately, the large bags had sturdy wheels because they felt heavy as hell as I towed them over the bumps toward the cottage. Rhonda pulled the carry-on with her right hand and balanced her load by hanging the purse over her left shoulder.

"How'd you find the phone number where I'm staying?" I asked.

"I remembered you said you were staying in Oak Bluffs with a relative of the cartoonist that Harry threw the party for," she said. "I looked through some of Harry's stuff while he was out drinking with his fat, ugly friend and found the cartoonist's name. Then I called information and asked for anyone with the last name of Jerome in Oak Bluffs. Lucky me. There was only one."

"You did get lucky."

She nodded. "Speaking of getting lucky, was I good the other night? I was so boozed up I don't remember much except your body coming over me on the bed like a big, warm blanket."

"You were great," I said. Sometimes a lie is much kinder than the truth.

"I hope so," Rhonda said. "I'll be better tonight because I won't be half-smashed."

"We have to discuss how that's going to work. My best friend and his wife will be right across the hall."

"And you'll be embarrassed when I scream 'oh, god' or yell 'don't stop' over and over and over."

"Worse than embarrassed. I'm afraid that my friend's wife will report any bedtime activities to my sweetheart in Cape Verde. You have to stay out of sight and you have to be as quiet as the proverbial mouse."

"That's really the shits," Rhonda said. "I don't know if I can screw without screaming. Especially at the end if I have a really good one."

"Guess I'll either have to gag you or sleep in the chair," I said, assuming it would be the latter.

"I've never done it with a gag in my mouth. I couldn't give you any tongue but I might really get off on it, like the time I sat on the guy's lap while he was driving with both of us naked on the freeway to Duluth."

"I thought you could only do it in the dark."

"He kept the dash lights off," she said. "And I kept my eyes shut the whole time."

Not wishing to hear any further details of Rhonda's high school sex life, I changed the subject to her plans for the future. How long was she planning to stay on the Vineyard?

"I'll stay as long as you'll let me," she said. "Even if I have to be gagged every night."

"I'm leaving early Saturday," I said, fudging the time by 24 hours. I wasn't sure how long I could keep this woman invisible and inaudible.

I'd been worried about my friends possibly walking out of the movie early, so I was relieved to find no lights showing at the cottage when we arrived. With Rhonda close behind me, I dragged the two heavy bags up the stairs and into my room. When I turned around, she had stripped off her tube top and was pulling down her shorts, confirming my suspicion that she wasn't wearing panties.

"How about I take a shower and we have a quickie in the dark before your friends get back?" she said, cupping her breasts in her hands. She spread her knees apart to display the space targeted by the tip of the spear and gave her hips a lewd wiggle. This titillation gave birth to a normal male reaction and Rhonda reached out and touched the tip of the tent with her index finger.

"Looks like you're all ready for action," she said. "Where can I take a quick shower?"

I pointed and said the bathroom was across the hall. She turned and walked out into the hall, giving her butt a provocative wiggle with each step. When she opened the bathroom door, I was surprised to see that the light was on. We'd all been very diligent about not running up Walt's electric bill.

Rhonda padded barefoot into the bathroom, gave a shriek, spun around and came running out. Her blue eyes were wide with fright.

"There's a naked man in the shower," she said, pressing her naked body tight against me with her arms clamped around my neck.

Looking over Rhonda's shoulder, I saw the shower curtain slide sideways and the naked man step out. He paused a moment to appreciate Rhonda's bare backside before he spoke.

CHAPTER 19

THE NEW ARRIVAL

"Hot damn! This is the nicest welcome home I've ever had," said Walt Jerome. "But I suppose this little darling didn't get undressed for my benefit."

"Actually it was for mine," I said. "But you're welcome to enjoy the view."

Having enjoyed the view as long as he deemed appropriate, Walt excused himself and went back into the bathroom. He emerged with a blue bath towel wrapped around his waist.

I tried to disentangle myself from Rhonda, who was clinging like a barnacle to a boat hull. "It's okay, Rhonda," I said. "Turn around and meet our host, Mr. Walter Jerome."

Slowly, she released her death grip from my neck, unwrapped her right leg from behind my left thigh and turned to face Walt.

"Rhonda this Walt; Walt this is Rhonda," I said.

"Hi, Rhonda," Walt said. His eyes moved vertically from her head to her toes, with a couple of brief stops along the way. "It's a pleasure to see...uh, to meet you."

"Likewise," Rhonda said. "Sort of like meeting somebody on Lucy Vincent Beach."

"Is that where you got the, uh, generous suntan?" Walt asked.

"That's where I first met her," I said. "You should go there next time you hide. The birds there are much prettier than your piping plovers."

"Do they all have so little plumage?" he asked. His roaming eyes had stopped at the level of the dark, slender spear.

"My research was limited by my proximity to this specimen," I said.

"Would you two bird watchers mind if I went in and took my shower now?" Rhonda asked.

"Fly away," I said.

"Let me clear my stuff out of there before you perch," Walt said. He went into the bathroom and returned carrying his cut-off jeans and a pair of sandals. Rhonda zipped in and closed the door with a bang.

"Guess I scared your chick," Walt said. "I hope it doesn't fowl up your evening." I groaned and decided I was going to like this man.

Walt joined me minutes later on the porch. He'd put on some faded blue-jeans cutoffs and a T-shirt that had been used to wipe up several colors of spilled paint. He was carrying two bottles of Bass Ale that Dave had put in the refrigerator.

Walt held one bottle out to me, whereupon I recited my usual speech about being an alcoholic and displayed the bottle of root beer I was consuming. He said he'd find a use for the extra bottle of ale.

"Where is everybody?" he asked as he settled into a wicker chair.

"They went to the new pirate movie downtown," I said. "I've already seen it. It's a dog."

"And instead of watching a dog, you picked up a dolly. Good for you."

"Actually, that's not exactly what happened." I replayed the events that led up to the surprise meeting of their bare bodies in the bathroom.

"You scared me as much as you did her," I said. "The house looked dark from the outside and we've had some nasty visitors lately."

"The window in that bathroom is blocked off because old Mrs. Oswald next door complained that she could see me naked from her bathroom window, which faces mine."

"Couldn't you also see her?"

"No way. In fact, she had to stand on a stepstool to see me. Ray caught her looking so she had to complain."

"So, where have you been the last few days?" I asked.

"Staying with a friend who lives in the woods on a narrow little dirt track off South Road in Chilmark. Not too far from that Lucy Vincent Beach your little brown-skinned chicky loves so well."

"We've been hunting for you. We were going to capture Dolly and try to get her to tell us where you went."

"She didn't know. I snuck through Oak Bluffs in the middle of the night and left her a note so she wouldn't haul any more food out to Chappy."

"Have you heard that Charles Morgan's been charged with the murder?"

"My friend is rustic, but he's got a TV. That's why I decided it was safe to come home."

I told him that the police still wanted to talk to him and he said he'd call Detective Gouveia in the morning. He was finishing the second bottle of ale when we heard voices and saw four dark forms approaching in the moonlight.

The moviegoers were as surprised and delighted to see Walt as I had been. Well, not quite as surprised. There was a scene of hugs and hubbub, everybody got another cold drink and we sat and talked until after midnight.

We might have yakked on even longer if Carol hadn't decided to turn in. She said goodnight and went upstairs, causing the rest of us to rise and begin moving toward our respective bedrooms. We were frozen by the sound of a female shriek.

"That's Carol," Al said.

Another female shriek, but a different voice. "Oh, shit," I said. Everyone was looking at me when Carol returned to the porch towing a scared-looking blonde clad only in a white bath towel.

"Look what I found reading a magazine in the bathroom," Carol said.

All eyes turned to Carol and her captive. All eyes turned back to me, looking for an explanation. I felt my face get very warm.

I managed to introduce Rhonda Fairchild to the group, give a hasty explanation of her plight and concoct a quick story about me moving to the daybed on the side porch so she could have my room for the night. Somehow, I got the feeling that nobody was buying this story.

Plunging on, I asked Rhonda why she was reading in the bathroom instead of in the bedroom I'd given to her.

"There's a cat in that bedroom," Rhonda said. "I'm allergic to cats. I wasn't in there five minutes before my eyes started to water and my nose started running. So I went and sat on the john."

"Were you planning to spend the night there?" I asked.

"No, silly, I was waiting for you to come up and show me some other place to sleep," she said.

"Wearing nothing but a towel?" Carol asked.

"I don't usually wear anything to bed," Rhonda said. Al was struck with a sudden coughing fit and Dave turned away to study a wisp of cloud that given the moon a mustache. Cindy pursed her lips and gave me nod that said I'd been caught like a kid with his hand in the cookie jar.

Trying to maintain my pretense of innocent benevolence, I suggested that Rhonda take the aforementioned daybed, but Walt said he'd be happy to sleep there instead of the downstairs bedroom, where he'd dropped his stuff when he found all three upstairs bedrooms occupied. This would leave the downstairs bedroom, which was adjacent to the sleeping porch, open for Rhonda. Walt gallantly offered to dig out some sheets and make up the bed in that room. Rhonda said that was a lot of trouble and that she could sleep on the daybed. Walt said he wouldn't hear of such a thing when there was a proper guestroom available.

Carol escorted Rhonda upstairs and Rhonda returned a few minutes later wearing pink shorty pajamas, which I assumed were on loan from Carol. Walt appeared from the back bedroom and said everything was ready. We all said goodnight and filed out of the living room.

As I was leaving, Rhonda caught my shoulder with one hand and my butt with the other. "Come back downstairs and gag me when everybody's asleep," she whispered. "I'll take off Carol's jammies before I lay down."

"Better leave them on in case I can't find a gag," I said. I had no intention of returning with or without a gag.

"You're not coming back, are you?" she said.

"It just won't work. Walt's sure to hear us, and the way everything creaks in this old house they might even hear us upstairs."

"Chicken shit! Chicken shit!"

"Cluck, cluck." I pried her fingers off my right buttock and almost ran to the stairs.

Al was in the hallway, near the door to my bedroom. "That was pretty quick thinking," he said.

"Whatever do you mean?" I asked.

"You sleeping in the side porch while the bare-ass blonde's in your bed? Give me a break."

"I'll give you a break in the neck if you talk like that in front of Carol."

"No need for violence, Romeo. Carol's already broken your crackpot story." He disappeared into their bedroom.

In my room, I found Sherlock Holmes stretched on his left side across the bed with his back against the pillows. He opened his eyes, raised his head an inch and opened his mouth two inches in a toothy yawn.

"Some friend you are," I said. "You just spoiled a sure thing." On the other hand, maybe that was a good thing.

★ ★ ★

I was half awake Thursday morning when I heard a tap, tap tapping at my chamber door. Being fairly certain that it was not a raven, I crawled out of bed, pulled on a pair of under shorts to cover my bare bottom and opened the door. In trotted Rhonda, still wearing Carol's "jammies."

"Mind if I get dressed?" she said. "I have to do it quick because of your old cat."

"Go right ahead," I said, settling back onto the bed.

Rhonda put on a performance, whipping off the pajamas with the flare of a dance club stripper, twirling her body in a naked pirouette and giving me a full moon shot as she bent over to pull some clothes out of a bag on the floor. She straightened and turned toward me while she snuggled her boobs into a bra and ever-so-slowly pulled a pair of see-through panties up her legs and over the shaft of the spear. While she was mooning me, I'd put a pillow on my lap, thus denying her the pleasure of seeing the advanced state of tumescence her reverse-strip show had inspired.

She finished her act by putting on a pair of shorts and a scoop-neck blouse. "See you downstairs, chicken shit," she said as she bounced out the door.

I lay back down and my hand came in contact with the cause of Rhonda's affliction. As I absently-mindedly scratched behind Sherlock Holmes's ears, I replayed the events of the previous evening. Suddenly, I stopped scratching and sat up straight, causing Sherlock to leap away and assume a defensive posture with the hair on his tail standing out like bristles on a bottle brush.

"Sorry, Sherlock," I said. "But I've got work to do." Walt had reappeared last night and I had to report this to Don O'Rourke. I fired up the laptop and, sitting on the bed in my underwear, composed and sent off a story about the missing former editor waltzing into his house unannounced and causing consternation—I didn't get specific about his close encounter with Rhonda Fairchild—among the temporary residents.

In less than two minutes I had a reply from my city editor. "Good work. Get more detail and quotes for tomorrow's paper. Also current pix of Walt." I swallowed the temptation to remind Don once again that I was theoretically on vacation and meekly replied, "OK."

When I went downstairs a few minutes later, I found Cindy and Carol making pancakes for all. Cindy gave me a quick "good morning" as I dug out a can of cat food, but Carol looked the other way. Al had been right; Carol had broken my crackpot story.

There were seven of us for breakfast on the porch. Rhonda chatted up the other three men and avoided eye contact with me like a millionaire passing a homeless street person. Cindy and Carol sat off by themselves, not speaking either to me or Rhonda. Shunned like an Amish backslider, I contemplated taking my plate up to my room to commune with Sherlock, but I stayed where I wasn't wanted, silently watching a succession of fluffy cumulus clouds drift across the blue Vineyard sky. One could almost become weary of day after day of such idyllic weather.

After breakfast, Rhonda picked up the phone book and went off in a corner with her cell phone to look for a hotel room. Carol and Cindy said they wanted to go for a walk and Al and Dave said they'd go with them. Walt said he'd go talk to Detective Gouveia. I said I'd tag along, hoping to be allowed to interview Charles Morgan for my freelance piece. It was a long shot, but if I could be perceived as delivering Walt to the police station, the detective might return the favor by taking me to see Morgan.

The tit-for-tat worked with Gouveia. The only hitch was getting Morgan to agree to see me. After some discussion with the detective, Morgan acquiesced on two conditions—he wouldn't answer questions he didn't like and I wouldn't tape record the discussion.

Morgan was his usual charming self, scowling through the bars at every question and growling out his answers in that gravelly voice. I started low-key by asking him where he was from originally.

"I grew up in Fa'haven," he said. "But I was livin' in New Beffa when Wade come lookin' for an experienced diver." I wondered how to spell those cities and where I'd find them on the map.

We went on to talk about his background as a diver, which was impressive, and segued into his arrangement with Wade Waters, which Morgan described as a "50-50 deal." The session ended when I asked him about the day Waters disappeared.

"I don't care what anybody says, I didn't kill Wade," he said. "That bartender and that waitress are both lyin' through their teeth, and I don't know why. Now fuck off, I've told you all I'm gonna say." He turned his back to me and walked over to his toilet, where I heard him unzip his fly.

I thanked him and…well, walked off.

On the way back to the cottage, I asked Walt about the spelling and location of Fa'haven and New Beffa.

"That would be native New England speak for Fairhaven and New Bedford," he said. "They're both busy seaports. Big fishing towns. I'll point them out on the map when we get back."

When we reached the cottage, we found Rhonda getting into a taxi. She announced that Harry Dick had forgiven her and she was going back to Summer Sweet because he said he missed her. Her final words to me were, "So long, chicken shit." She even flipped me the bird through the window as the taxi drove away.

"You seem to have offended the young lady in some way," Walt said.

"She wanted me to come back down and play hide the weenie with her after everybody else went to bed last night," I said.

"We'd have both gotten a bang out of that. I was awake for at least an hour after you guys all went upstairs."

"I told her we'd have an audience, but she's in show business and didn't seem to care who was listening."

I got my laptop and sat on the porch typing in the quotes I'd jotted down during my interview with Morgan. As I resumed putting the story together, I was bothered by the discrepancy between his claim that he'd been served a drink while waiting for a friend in the Circuit Avenue bar and the statements given to police by the bartender and the waitress, who said they'd never seen him. Always the thorough reporter, I decided to try to question the bartender and the waitress.

A call to Gouveia got me their names, on the cross-my-heart promise that I'd never tell anyone that he was my source. "They're both new here this summer from Brazil," he said. "I ain't even sure they're legal, but that ain't none of my business."

It was getting close to lunch time, so Walt said he'd go with me and get a sandwich and a beer. The quartet of walkers had not returned and we decided they'd probably settled down to rest on the town beach.

"Give me a minute," Walt said. He went inside and returned a few minutes later. He had replaced the ratty shorts he'd worn at breakfast with a clean, nearly new pair. He'd also put on a flower-patterned aloha shirt and a pair of sandals. It was the first time I'd ever seen anything on Walt's feet.

The Gray Goose Bar and Grill was as dark as a gander's gullet inside and nearly devoid of customers. There were several tables available, but we sat at the right-hand end of the bar, which was long enough to accommodate seven stools. Walt ordered a beer, and I asked the straggly-haired bartender for a ginger ale with no ice. When the bartender, who didn't look old enough to be serving booze, set our drinks in front of us, I asked if his name was Adamo.

His chin jerked upward and he blinked nervously before he answered in the affirmative. I told him I was a writer doing a story on the mysterious murder of Wade Waters and said I'd like to ask him a couple of questions.

"The police say I shouldn't talk to no reporters," Adamo said.

"This isn't for a daily newspaper or even the island weekly," I said. "If I sell this story to a magazine it won't be published for several months. The trial might even be over by the time people read it."

Adamo thought about it while he walked away and mixed a gin and tonic for customer at the other end of the bar. When he came back to us, he asked, "What you want to know?"

"I want to know if you are absolutely certain that the accused man, Charles Morgan, was not in here at any time on the day Wade Waters disappeared."

"I tol' the police I never saw the man," Adamo said.

"Did you actually get a look at the man they've accused?"

"They take me to the jail and I look at four men through glass. I don' see none of them before."

"You're positive? You'll testify in court under oath that you never saw Charles Morgan in this room?"

"If I gotta," he said.

"You will gotta," I said. "What about the waitress? The one named Rita? Is she here?"

"She don' come in till six o'clock. She don' see this man here either."

"Did she go to the jail and look at the men behind the glass?"

"Yes, sir, she did. And she don' know any of them." He hurried away to open a beer for a man who'd taken the stool at the middle of the bar.

Adamo didn't come near us again until Walt waved an empty glass. We ordered cheeseburgers and fries, and Walt had a second beer. We ate slowly, hoping to get another shot at quizzing Adamo, but he stayed at the far end of the bar until Walt signaled for the check. Adamo approached us, stopped an arm's length away from Walt, dropped the check like it was burning his fingers and almost ran back his haven at the other end of the bar. We left a tip that would make Adamo feel better about talking to us and went back out into the sunlight, which was like facing a spotlight upon emerging from a cave.

"The bartender is lying," Walt said.

"I had that feeling, too," I said. Adamo's dark eyes had never connected with mine all the time I was quizzing him.

"I've interviewed hundreds, maybe thousands, of people in my time and I know when somebody is flat out lying to me."

"Me, too. The question is, why is he lying?"

"People lie to protect either themselves or somebody else. He sure as hell didn't have anything to do with the murder, so who would he be protecting?"

"If we answer that question, we might set Charles Morgan free."

"For which I'm sure he'll be forever grateful."

"I won't hold my breath waiting for a thank you card," I said.

"What's next?" Walt asked. The answer to that question was waiting for us on the porch of his cottage.

CHAPTER 20

CODE BUSTERS

"Welcome home, Walt," said Buck Studwell, rising from the most comfortable rocker on the porch. "Long time, no see."

"It's been a few years," Walt said. "What brings you back to the Vineyard, as if I didn't know?"

"Something you've got that I'd like to see," Buck said. "I'm willing to share whatever it leads to."

"If you're talking about Wade's chart, the cops have it," Walt said. He waved toward me. "Apparently Mr. Morgan took it rather forcibly from my young friend here. Have you met Mr. Mitchell?"

"I have," Buck said. "Mr. Mitchell and your nephew and a third guy all claim they never made a copy of the chart but I don't believe they're that stupid. And like I said, I'm willing to share whatever comes up from the Daniel French once I've cracked the code and found the wreck."

"We've already turned down a pretty fair bid from the Bottoms Up skipper," I said. "How much are you offering?"

"Then you admit you did make a copy?" Buck said.

"Maybe we did and maybe we didn't. I can't say either yea or nay, but when my friends come back we'll be glad to listen to you."

"You'd damn well better listen to me," Buck said. "If you

turned down that bastard Oberman, he's liable to come back here with something that talks louder than money."

I was thinking about Oberman's parting shot when we heard a shout from the sidewalk, heralding the return of the walking four. Soon we were all seated in a semi-circle, waiting to hear Buck Studwell's pitch.

Buck started low, as I expected, and we went through the offer-and-counteroffer routine until he reached a figure slightly above Dirk Oberman's take-it-or-leave-it level. "Thirty thousand upfront and 20 percent of whatever the treasure brings in is tops," Buck said. "Plus, I'll bust that code for you. If that's not good enough, you can go deal with Oberman."

The six of us exchanged looks. Walt tilted his head to the right, toward Buck. "Why don't you take about a 10-minute walk while we talk things over," Walt said.

Buck rose, looked at his wristwatch and said he'd be back in exactly 10 minutes. When he was out of earshot, our conference began.

"How do we know he has any right to the treasure?" Carol asked.

"We don't," Walt said. "But if anybody does, it's him. He claims that he still owns a piece of the All That Glitters, and we can ask to see proof of that."

"Morgan also claims part ownership," I said. "If Morgan's not convicted, the All That Glitters is at least part his, and he has the advantage that the wreck was found on his watch."

"I see a nasty court fight if Morgan turns out to be innocent," Cindy said. "We might come away with zero."

"But if they wind up splitting the booty, we'll still get a percentage of Studwell's percentage," Dave said. "And if we get his thirty-thou upfront, that's five-K apiece for doing basically nothing."

"On the other hand, we could be signing a pact with the devil," I said. "I'm not convinced that Studwell couldn't have been the killer, even though he claims he didn't get to the island until after Waters disappeared."

"Do you think Gouveia could check out Studwell's travel schedule?" Al asked.

"I'm sure he could," I said. "The question is, *would* Gouveia check out Studwell's travel schedule? The cops seem quite content to pin the killing on Morgan without looking at anybody else."

"That's the easy way out for them," Dave said.

"Two things if we decide to deal with Studwell," Al said. "Number one, we should push Gouveia to check on the guy's flights. In fact, he may have already done that. Number two, we should get everything we want from Studwell in writing."

Dave turned to his uncle. "Know any contract lawyers on the island?"

"Of course I do," Walt said. "When you're the editor of the local paper, you get to know everybody."

"We don't have to bring in the lawyer yet," Carol said. "Let's collect the $30,000, put it in Walt's bank account and let Mr. Studwell go to work on the code."

"I wonder if he's got $30,000," I said.

"Better make it a cashier's check," Cindy said.

We batted the ball back and forth for a few more minutes before reaching a decision. Buck Studwell was within 30 feet of the porch steps when we agreed unanimously to ask him for a cashier's check and to deposit same before showing him the chart. If Buck was able to break the code, Walt would call his lawyer and we'd tie up our percentage of the treasure's value nice and legal. Subject, of course, to the results of Charles Morgan's eventual day in court and any subsequent charges, such as first-degree murder, lodged against Buck Studwell.

Buck laughed when we explained the procedure. "You think I'm not good for a stinking 30 grand?" he said. "Let's go to the bank right now. I'll have them suck it out of my account electronically and hand you your lousy cashier's check to show you how grateful I am that you suddenly located a copy of the chart."

"Fair enough," Walt said. "Dave and I will go with you."

Off they went, like Dorothy's three friends following the yellow brick road. They were barely out of sight when Cindy dashed to the kitchen and came back with the brown paper bag from the freezer. She opened it, pulled out the envelope and peeked in to make sure the chart was still there. "We'll have it thawed and ready for Studwell to study the minute he comes back," she said.

"He should think this chart is really cool," I said.

"Let's hope the trail to the treasure hasn't grown cold," Al said.

★ ★ ★

Walt and Dave were smiling and Buck Studwell was wearing a blank expression when the trio of bank depositors reappeared.

"Break out the chart," Walt said. "Mr. Master Decoder has paid his dues and is ready to go to work."

Cindy spread the chart on a circular, glass-topped wicker table and we gathered around it. Buck looked at the markings and grunted.

There were two sets of upper case letters, each with 10 characters. We'd been assuming that one set was the code for latitude and the other for longitude, but both sets had too many characters to be a simple replacement code for degrees, minutes and seconds.

"He threw in some extra letters to fuck it up," Buck said. "If it was straight latitude and longitude coordinates, he'd only need six in each line."

"We've figured out that much," Walt said. "But there's no way of guessing which letters mean something and what letter stands for which number."

"Okay," Buck said. "We know the general area of the wreck is 41 degrees and about 20 minutes north and 70 degrees and between 15 and 25 minutes west. If we figure out what letter stands for four and what letter stands for seven, something might pop out and bite us."

The top line was WMHDCSPRIV. The second was NLCGCTFAYB.

"The letter C appears three times," Carol said. "It's the only letter that gets repeated." This is a woman who solves the Sudoku puzzle in the newspaper every morning.

"So how does that help us?" Dave asked. This is a cartoonist who occasionally needs to have his spelling corrected before his work is okayed for publication.

"We know that the latitude is 41 degrees. The minutes of longitude could fall into the teens, which would begin with a one," Carol said.

"And the minutes of latitude could be 21 or a wee bit less than 20, putting it in the teens," Buck said. "Let's try it with the Cs as ones."

Now we had WMHD1SPRIV and NL1G1TFAYB.

"Assuming the first set is latitude like it's generally written, we could make the D into a four," Buck said.

That gave us WMH41SPRIV.

"Say the S is a two and the R is a zero," Carol said. "That gives us WMH4120RIV. The problem now is figuring out what R and I equal to give us the seconds, assuming the V is just there as a decoy."

"I don't like it," Buck said. "Why would he pile three useless letters on the front end and only one on the back?"

"Added confusion?" I suggested.

"It ain't like Wade to do that," Buck said. "He was a very picky person when it came to balance. Always had everything centered on his boats so they were perfectly stable in the water."

"What if he put the longitude first as a trick?" Carol said. "What if we go to the second set and make L the four?"

Now we had N41G1TFAYB on that line.

"The T could be an eight or a nine," Buck said. "A seven would give us 17 minutes and put the wreck practically in downtown Nantucket."

"A nine would give us N41G19FAYB," Carol said.

"That's a real possibility," Walt said. "But figuring out the seconds is going to be a bitch. We'll need Lady Luck on our shoulder for those."

"Holy shit!" Buck yelled. "I think I've got it."

We responded with a six-voice chorus of, "What?"

"Lady Luck," he said. "Carly Smith!"

"Wade's girlfriend?" I asked. "The woman who drowned?"

"What's she got to do with it?" Dave asked.

"It figures that Wade would work that way," Buck said. "Try it with C as one, A as two, R as three and so on, with H as a zero. Just skip all the letters that aren't in the name Carly Smith."

Carol wrote them out: W70D16P38V and N41G19F25B.

"That's it!" Buck said. "70 degrees, 16 minutes and 38 seconds west and 41 degrees, 19 minutes, 25 seconds north. That's where the fucking Daniel French lies."

After a round of celebratory whoops, somebody asked Buck what would happen next.

"I round up a couple of divers and a boat, and we go check out that spot," he said.

"You can't use the All That Glitters," I said. "It's still wrapped up in yellow crime scene tape."

"I'll rent something to take out there for a look-see. Then if the wreck is really there, I'll need a proper treasure hunting boat. Maybe I can persuade the cops to unwrap the one that belongs to me."

"You're claiming the All That Glitters?" Walt said.

"Damn right. I've got paper that says I still own half that boat. If Morgan claims he owns half, it's Wade's half, not mine."

"With luck, Morgan will be out of the picture for the rest of his life," Dave said.

Walt said he'd contact a lawyer in the morning and set up a time to meet and put the details of our agreement into writing. Buck gave Walt his cell phone number and told him to call when the meeting was scheduled. "Most any day next week is good," he said.

"Let us know when you're going out to check the spot," Walt said. "I want to go with you."

"Make it tomorrow or Saturday, and we'll all go," Dave said. I wasn't so sure that I wanted to be a part of the group, but I didn't say anything.

"Might be tough getting a boat on a Saturday, but I'll see what I can do," Buck said. "Ladies and gentlemen, it's been a pleasure to do business with you." He waved and walked away toward downtown Oak Bluffs.

We were still exchanging high-fives and singing a chorus of "15 men on a dead man's chest" when the familiar black sedan drove up. Dirk Oberman hoisted his 300 pounds out of the front passenger seat and walked slowly up the porch steps, which creaked in protest at every footfall. "Somebody win the lottery?" he asked.

"You might say that," Walt said. "We just miraculously found a copy of the elusive chart and cut a deal for a percentage of the Daniel French treasure with somebody who doesn't look like you."

"Really?" Oberman said. "What does he look like?"

"He looks like somebody who made us a better offer," Walt said.

"Not Buck Studwell?"

"Maybe yes and maybe no," Walt said. "It's really none of your business now that you've been outbid."

Oberman stared at Walt, clenching and unclenching his fists. Walt met the stare until the big man looked away, sweeping his gaze across all of us.

"You made a real big mistake, Mr. Jerome," he said. "And so did Buck Studwell."

"Maybe and maybe not," Walt said. "We'll mention your comments to the Oak Bluffs police, so they'll know where to look if anything unusual happens to any of us."

"Fuck the Oak Bluffs police," Oberman said. "And fuck all of you too, so-called ladies included." He turned and strode back to the black sedan.

"Oh!" Cindy wailed, loud enough for Oberman to hear. "I think I'm going to swoon." We all waved a smartass goodbye as the black sedan drove away. Thirty grand can make people awfully damn cocky.

We decided to spend some our newly-acquired wealth that evening in a restaurant on the harbor in Edgartown. With Walt driving, we crammed all six of us into the little sedan and made the trip. Al kept watch out the rear window and reported no followers.

The dining room was on the second story, and our table provided a gorgeous view of the harbor. We watched a huge catamaran called the Krazy Karl depart full of passengers for a sunset cruise, which reminded me that its owner, Henry Agnew, had lied to me about his relationship with the late Wade Waters. I still wanted to talk to the man about that.

While the others were having a round of drinks, I excused myself and went out on the open-air deck to make a call to Martha Todd. I couldn't wait any longer to tell her about my easy-come money because it was almost 11 p.m. in Cape Verde. After three rings, something went click and a recorded voice said, "We're sorry, but the number you are calling is not in service."

CHAPTER 21

WHERE'S MARTHA?

"Probably a glitch in the system," Al said. "There's no way Martha wouldn't pay the phone bill."

"Service might have been knocked out by a storm or something," Carol said.

"Or she might have moved to a better apartment," Dave said.

"Why would she move three months before she can come home?" I asked. Actually, I had a theory on why she'd change, but I didn't want to think or talk about it. My theory started and ended with the word *Frederico*.

"Do you have her office number?" Al asked. "You could try calling her there tomorrow."

"I have, and I will," I said. The thought of the answer I might receive put a damper on the celebration dinner for me. While the other five drank wine and chattered over their grilled swordfish and broiled scallops, I spent an hour nibbling at a plate of deep-fried shrimp and wishing I could drown my anxiety in a couple of vodka tonics. Being a recovering alcoholic isn't for sissies.

"Will you folks be having dessert tonight?" Brenda, our server, asked as she began clearing away the wreckage. If I hadn't been feeling so gloomy, I'd have noticed that she was wearing an open-neck blouse that exposed a substantial acreage of suntanned cleavage. But, being deep in the dumps, I paid no attention to Brenda's bosom.

"We'll have what we ordered when we came in," Walt said. I wasn't aware that we'd ordered anything, but before I could ask Walt what he was talking about, two more servers appeared bearing a chocolate cake with two large white candles blazing on top.

"Happy birthday, Mitch," Walt said.

"Oh, my god," I said. "It is, isn't it? I forgot what day it was."

The cake was set down, and I was instructed to make a wish and blow out the candles. One was shaped like the number four, the other like a zero.

The wish was obvious: Find Martha. The blowout was easy. What the hell, it was only two candles. I was now officially 40 years old.

"Who remembered that my birthday was on the 13th?" I asked.

"Who the hell do you think," Al said. "Who could forget that kind of bad luck? For your parents, I mean."

I felt much better eating cake and the ice cream that accompanied it. I even took note of Brenda's charming cleavage when she leaned over Walt's shoulder to present the check. Because it was my birthday, I was not allowed to contribute to the pot, but I slipped a $10 bill under my empty cake plate as a personal token of appreciation to Brenda.

Being the only one free of alcohol, I drove us home despite my advanced age. During the ride, we were all in high spirits, making plans to spend our loot and hoping like hell that our hero, Buck Studwell, didn't turn out to be the villain who killed Wade Waters. Dave and Cindy said they'd take their next vacation in Ireland to explore the land of Dave's ancestors. Carol was eager for a trip to Norway to do likewise, but Al was more interested in a warm-weather cruise. Walt said he'd like to go through the Panama Canal.

"What're you going to with your five grand?" Al asked.

"Go to Hawaii," I said. "On a honeymoon, I hope. That's if I can ever find Martha."

This brought a round of cheers and a chorus of assurances that Martha would be communicating with me anon.

Unfortunately, the celebratory air was fouled by the first of two messages we found on Walt's answering machine when we returned to the cottage. Walt pushed the button and heard a familiar male voice. "Jeez, Walt, I'm surprised that all of you went away and left your shack standing empty," Dirk Oberman said. "You know how easy it would be for something bad to happen to the place when there's nobody home? An electric short or a little old spark of some kind could turn you into a homeless man."

"That son of a bitch," Walt said. "Save that message for Detective Gouveia."

"From now on, we'll have to leave a rear guard here every time we go some place," Dave said.

"We're going home Sunday," Cindy said. "Who will you get to watch the place?"

"Don't worry about it," Walt said. "I'll find somebody. If nothing else I'll hire an off-duty cop."

The second message was also a familiar voice, this one female and not nearly so threatening. "Mitch, honey, I want to apologize for being such a shit," Rhonda Fairchild said. "Please give me a call so I can tell you I'm sorry." She rattled off a number but I didn't write it down.

"Need a pencil and paper?" Carol asked. The others had turned and politely walked away, but she was watching me like a teacher looking for cheaters on a test.

"I don't need to call her back," I said. "A recorded apology is plenty." Carol tossed her head in a gesture that said *bullshit* and left the kitchen. As soon as she was out of sight, I grabbed the pad and pen beside the phone, wrote Rhonda's number and tucked it into my shirt pocket. Better to return her call on my cell phone where nosy watchdogs couldn't hear.

In my bedroom, Sherlock Holmes greeted me with a meow and rolled onto his back looking for a belly rub. I administered the treatment, scratched behind his ears as a bonus and shivered at the thought of what could have happened to Sherlock if Dirk Oberman had created an electrical short or a spark in the cottage while we were away.

"I'll make damn sure there's somebody here to take care of you at all times," I said to Sherlock as I punched in Rhonda's number.

Rhonda repeated her apology. "Sometimes when a girl gets really horny she forgets that other people have sexual hang-ups," she said. "You were right about not doing it where all your friends could hear us."

I said I was glad she agreed and asked how things were going with her old pal, Harry.

"Everything's okay again," she said. "Harry's fat, ugly buddy found some hard-up bimbo who was willing to do him for 200 bucks, so he and Harry are both happy. I'm the only one that still needs to get laid."

"Sorry about that," I said.

"Why don't you come out here and take care of my needs right now?"

"Can't do it tonight." I thought of the possible bad news I might hear from Martha Todd in the morning and added, "Maybe tomorrow night."

"Maybe, shmaybe," Rhonda said. "I need you."

"Hang in there, kid," I said. "I'll call you if I'm coming."

"Don't come before you get here." She was still giggling at her own bit of wit when I said good night and punched off.

"Okay, Martha," I said, looking at my pillow. "If you've moved in with Frederico, I'm moving on with Fairchild." Sherlock, snoozing beside the pillow, raised his head, blinked his eyes twice and went back to sleep.

★ ★ ★

My hungry bed partner nudged me awake shortly after 8 a.m. Friday. I pulled on some khaki shorts and followed him to the kitchen. There was only one can of cat food on the shelf, which meant another trip to the store before our Sunday departure.

I scooped some of the fishy-smelling compound into Sherlock's dish, scattered some bits of dry cat food on top of it, filled his water bowl and went back up to my bedroom. It was 15 minutes past noon in Cape Verde. I picked up my cell phone. Did I really want to call Martha at her office? I put down my cell phone. She'd probably be having lunch right now. I'd wait another hour before calling.

Carol was making coffee when I returned to the kitchen. If she had any suspicion about my returning Rhonda's call surreptitiously, it wasn't evident from her greeting. While the coffee was dripping, we discussed such heavy topics as the weather and the probable temperature of the water at State Beach. The sun was shining in a cloudless sky again, making this the 14th consecutive day without rain. I was actually getting bored by day after day of sunshine, with only the passage of a stray cumulus cloud to cast an occasional shadow.

Eventually, all six of us were together on the porch drinking coffee and devouring an assortment of muffins and cinnamon rolls that Walt had procured on an early walk to the bakery.

"What's the plan of the day for the vacationers?" Walt asked when the coffee pot was dry. "I'm going to call Detective Gouveia and ask him to come listen to that bastard Oberman's phone message. And, after that, I'm going to call a lawyer and set up a meeting to put our agreement with Mr. Studwell on paper in iron-clad legalese."

"I'm going to put in some time on the freelance piece I'm trying to write about this alleged vacation," I said. Not wishing to evoke any further words of comfort, I decided not to reiterate my intention to call Martha's office.

"Hey, do you need any pix to go with that piece?" Al asked. "I've got a shit load of island shots in my camera and I'd like to cull out the losers today."

"Knowing your unparalleled skill as a photographer, I can't believe every exposure isn't perfect and precious," I said.

"Even the best of us takes an occasional shot that isn't worth the megabytes it's consuming," he said. "Sort of like a writer who has to delete an imperfect sentence now and then."

"Really? Do some writers have to do that?"

"So I'm told. Of course, the writers I know always write right."

"Right you are," I said. "Now run right up and get your camera and we'll hook it right to my laptop for a right fine slide show."

"Right-o," Al said. "I'll be right back."

"Right on." We both headed upstairs and to pick up our equipment.

The women wanted to drive to West Tisbury and watch the glass blowers at work in a shop that sold incredibly beautiful—and incredibly expensive—plates, goblets and vases. That's *vase* to rhyme with *bras*, not *vase* pronounced like *ace*. Dave said he'd go along and keep an eye out for our buddies from the Bottoms Up. Al and I told them to have fun and they left while we were setting up our slide show.

After a series of scenic shots and various pictures of our group, we were treated to views of the press conference at which the results of the Wade Waters autopsy were announced. As they flashed past, something surprising registered on my brain.

"Hey," I said. "Stop it and back up one frame."

The picture showed several faces in the crowd of media people listening to the DA. The face that had caught my attention was that of a slender, white-haired man who stood ramrod straight in the back of the pack.

"What's he doing there?" I asked, pointing at the man.

"Who is he?" Al asked.

"Henry Agnew. The guy who lied to me at the party about barely knowing Wade Waters. He's not a reporter. He owns a big catamaran and sailboat rental business out in Edgartown."

"Didn't you find out that he'd been in business with Waters? Maybe he was interested in how his ex-partner was killed."

"Yeah, I guess that makes sense. On with the show."

We looked at some more scenery and pictures of our group until we hit a series of shots taken at Charles Morgan's arraignment. As they were flipping by, Al said, "Hey, there he is again."

He stopped on a shot of people leaving the courtroom. Sure enough, there was Henry Agnew in the doorway.

"That settles it," I said. "I've been putting off talking to him about his little fairytale, but now I can't wait to ask him why he's got such a strong interest in a man he told me he didn't really know."

"That should get the conversation off to a pleasant start," Al said.

"I'm more interested in the finish than the start."

"Well, if you want a fair finish, don't let him give you a line."

We downloaded a couple of scenic shots, a view of the All That Glitters and one showing Morgan in the courtroom as possible illustrations for my freelance piece. Then I put the laptop away and again picked up my cell phone.

I sat on the bed and looked at the phone. Did I really want to do this? Yes, I told myself, I really do have to know what the hell is going on in Cape Verde. I punched in the number, listened to the recorded menu and punched in Martha's extension after the proper prompt.

Her phone rang four times before something clicked and I heard another recorded monotone message: "You have reached the voice mail of Martha Todd. Please leave a message after the tone and she will return your call as soon as possible."

I suppressed an expletive and waited for the tone. I tried to sound cheerful and casually curious as I said, "It's me. Please call me or send an e-mail and tell me why your phone's been disconnected. I've been e-mailing you and calling you at home. Love you. Bye now." I put the phone into my pocket and noticed that I was sweating more profusely than I could attribute to the temperature in the room.

With the Chevy gone to West Tisbury, I had a choice of Walt's rust-riddled Land Rover or my bike as a means of transportation to Edgartown. I chose the bike because it would be good exercise—as long as I didn't have to keep pace with Daffy Dolly—and because I was afraid of the damn Land Rover.

Wearing shorts and a T-shirt and a coating of sun screen, I started pedaling toward Beach Road, which led to the bike path. When I turned onto Beach Road and looked east, I was amazed to see a wall of gray clouds covering the sky ahead of me. This meant I wouldn't be baking in the sun all the way to Edgartown so I breathed a silent thank you to the weather gods.

I figured that Agnew's office must be near where I'd seen the Krazy Karl start out the previous evening. This meant braving the traffic for several blocks down Edgartown's main street after the bike path turned toward South Beach and Katama. I arrived at the harbor unscathed, having had only one brief incident involving a Mercedes SUV with a typically-aggressive Massachusetts driver.

Following signs on the dock, I found the office of Agnew Sailing Vessels, Ltd., in a weathered wooden building facing the harbor. A young woman seated at a desk facing the door greeted me with a smile worthy of a TV toothpaste commercial and asked if she could help me. Below the smile, she wore a gold bikini top that barely contained a pair of suntanned boobs that would have stood out among the crowd at Hooters. I wanted to say, "How can thee help me? Let me count the ways."

Instead, I asked to see Mr. Agnew.

"I'm sorry, he's not in today," she said. "He had business to take care of off-island."

"Will he be in tomorrow?" Saturday would be my last chance to ask him why he'd lied.

"Yes, I believe he will." Again, she flashed the whiter-than-white smile.

"What time would be best to catch him?"

"I'd say real early, before we open for customers at nine o'clock. After that, he's very busy checking out boats."

I thanked her, received another dazzling smile in return and retreated, walking sideways like a crab so that I could catch a last, lingering look at the teeny weenie gold bikini.

Now what? I was in Edgartown on business without anyone to conduct business with. As I was about to get on my bike, I remembered that the newspaper office was just a couple of blocks away. Maybe my friend Terry Shaw would be in. She might enlighten me further about Henry Agnew.

A pleasant, middle-aged woman at the front desk told me that Terry was not in. I thanked the woman and turned to leave. I was almost out the door when another idea popped into my head and I returned to the desk.

"Would it be possible to look at some back issues?" I asked. "Say from 10 years ago or so?"

"I'm sorry, sir. We only allow members our staff or other media personnel to use our files," she said.

I hauled out my billfold, opened it to the plastic window containing my St. Paul press pass and held it out for her to see. She studied the photo, looked at my face and nodded. "Right this way, Mr. Mitchell. I'll set you up with whatever dates you'd like to see."

A few minutes later, I was seated in front of a screen, scrolling through a spool of microfilm. I had asked for films from 11 and 10 years ago in hope of finding something pertaining to the partnership of Henry Agnew and Wayne Waters and the departure of Waters from the Vineyard.

It was a tiresome chore, hard on both the eyes and the butt. I zipped through the first year fairly quickly and slowed down on the second because that was the year Terry had said Waters had left for Florida. After mid-May, I saw ads for Agnew & Waters Water Sports in every issue until late August, when Waters' name no longer appeared in the copy and the name changed to Agnew Sailing Vessels, Ltd.

Wondering if I'd passed over any news stories about Agnew & Waters, I rewound the film all the way back to January and started the year over again. In an April edition, I spotted a headline that stopped me cold. The story below the headline wasn't what I'd been expecting to find, but it told me something about the reason for Wayne Waters' abrupt abandonment of his job and his home. Now I really needed to talk to Henry Agnew in the morning.

I printed a copy of the page, folded it and tucked it into my right rear pocket. Then I rewound the film, shut off the machine and returned the spools to the woman at the desk. When I went out to unlock my bike from the railing beside the steps, it was raining. As I mopped off the seat with the tail of my T-shirt, I thought of the old warning: Be careful what you wish for; you might get it.

The faster I pedaled, the harder it rained. By the time I reached the shelter of Walt's cottage, I was begging for a return of the constant, boring sunshine. My hair was plastered to my scalp, water was pouring down my face and neck, and my clothes were beyond saturation. On the front porch, I removed everything but my briefs, which were also soaked, and dashed toward the stairs, hoping that if the women were home they would be occupied in the kitchen.

No such luck. As I zipped through the living room, I heard two female voices.

"Hey, everybody, it's show time," said Carol Jeffrey.

"Nice buns," said Cindy Jerome. "How about an encore?"

"Not unless you stuff $20 bills into my waist band," I yelled as I took the stairs two at a time and ran into the shelter of my bedroom. When I slammed the door, Sherlock Holmes opened his eyes and raised his head off the bedspread. He stared at my dripping head and body for a moment, then laid back his ears and hissed, apparently mistaking me for some sort of creature that had slithered out of the sea.

"It's me, Sherlock," I said. My voice assured him that I was not an alien invader come to take away his resting place. The hissing stopped, the ears returned to their normal upright position, the head returned to its normal down position and the eyes returned to their normal position, which is closed. I grabbed some dry underwear out of the dresser and went across the hall to the bathroom to towel off and change.

When I was dry and comfortable again, I logged onto my laptop to check for a possible e-mail from Martha. She hadn't called my cell phone, which, incidentally, was still in the pocket of my waterlogged shorts on the porch. The glowing laptop monitor revealed that she hadn't sent an e-mail either, and it was well past time that she would have left her office.

"Where the hell are you?" I said as I shut down the computer.

Thoughts of Frederico were running through my head as I entered the living room on the way to the porch. Instantly, I was snapped back to reality by a chorus of catcalls from Carol and Cindy.

"Lousy encore!" Carol yelled.

"I've got a 20," Cindy shouted. "You promised to perform."

"Sorry, girls," I said. "Show's over. Union rules." I continued to the porch, where I retrieved my soggy wallet, the sopping copy of the news story and my wet cell phone. I wrung some of the water out of my T-shirt and shorts and poured half a cup of water out of each of my sneakers, wondering if I'd ever wear them again.

Hoping that my cell phone had survived its near drowning, I dug Rhonda Fairchild's number out of my billfold and punched it in. I was relieved to hear that my phone was working, but disappointed when all I got was Rhonda's voice mail.

"Help, help me, Rhonda," I said, mimicking the old Beach Boys' song. "Give me a call at this number." I recited my cell number and punched off, wondering if I really wanted her to return the call.

"Damn it, Martha," I said out loud. "Where the hell have you gone?"

CHAPTER 22

SEVERE DÉJÀ VU

Walt insisted on cooking supper for us that night. The rain halted abruptly and the sun burst forth at about 5:30, allowing him to use the grill on the back patio. He cooked a bluefish caught so recently that the gills had barely stopped moving, basting it with a sauce he'd gleaned from a book called "Blues," written by the late John Hershey, a former island summer resident. This was accompanied by a salad of assorted greens, tomatoes, peppers and scallions Walt had picked up fresh at a farm stand, and a loaf of whole wheat bread he'd baked while I was scrolling through the microfilm in the newspaper office.

This feast improved my emotional state somewhat, although I found myself wishing I could have some of the white wine the others were drinking with the meal. Like a good little alky, I made do with iced tea.

I kept my cell phone in my pocket hoping for a call from Martha, but when it finally rang, the caller was Rhonda. We were all sitting on the porch, eating Walt's homemade peanut butter cookies and drinking coffee, so I got up and walked around the corner of the house where I could talk in private.

"So, are we feeling horny tonight?" Rhonda asked. "Is that why we're calling little Rhonda?"

I wasn't sure whether I was horny or just pissed at Martha, but I told Rhonda, "Yes, we are."

Apparently, my lack of certainty was reflected in my voice because Rhonda said, "You don't sound like you'll die tonight if you don't reap the pleasures of my ripe, luscious body."

I remembered that ripe, luscious body walking toward me on Lucy Vincent Beach. "Do you want me to do some deep breathing?" I asked in a throaty whisper.

"I want you to sound like you really want to get down and dirty in the sack with me more than anything else in the world."

I remembered her ripe, luscious body spread-eagled on the bed at the Summer Sweet Inn with her brain gone numb in an alcoholic stupor. "I really want to do it with you more than anything in the world," I said in the same irresistible whisper. "I'm as horny as a satyr after six years on a deserted island."

"You're absolutely positive?" she asked.

I thought about the short-hair spear that pointed the way to Rhonda's ripe, luscious pudenda almost brushing against my face in the upstairs bedroom. "Absolutely positive."

"Cross your dick and hope to die?" she asked with a giggle.

"That, too," I said.

"Well, ain't that too damn bad?" said Rhonda. "It just so happens that I met a guy on the nude beach today whose picture would take up two pages in my book, if you know what I mean, and he's coming here tonight so I can sample in the dark what I saw in the daylight. I wanted you real bad last night and you blew me off, so you can go blow yourself off tonight, Mr. High-and-Mighty Mitchell." With that, the line went dead, leaving me wondering whether I should be pissed off, disappointed or relieved. I decided on a combination of all three.

"Was it Martha?" Al asked when I rejoined the group.

"No," I said. "It was nothing important." I told myself that this was true, that the only thing really important was my impending discussion with Henry Agnew. I decided not to mention either the surprising news story or my plan for an early-morning confrontation with Agnew to the others. I knew all three men would want to tag along, and I didn't think this interview would be successful if it were conducted by a committee of four.

However, I followed Al into the kitchen when he went to refill his coffee cup and showed him the page that I'd spread out to dry on a rack in the oven.

"Holy shit!" Al said when he saw the headline. "That explains a lot."

"It does," I said. "And I'm going to ask Agnew to explain a lot more first thing tomorrow morning."

"You're going to need backup."

"I think this is a one-man job. I'm afraid that too many inquisitors would spook the inquisitee."

"How about a silent partner?" Al asked. "Just in case the subject gets unfriendly."

"Make that silent and invisible and you're on," I said.

"Wake me when you get up," he said. "But don't rattle Carol's cage."

★ ★ ★

My alarm buzzed at 6 a.m. Sherlock Holmes raised his head long enough to give me a disapproving look and went back to sleep. I pulled on the underwear, shorts and T-shirt I'd changed into after my watery ride home and tip-toed barefoot into the Jeffreys' bedroom. I silently nudged Al awake and retreated to my room to put on a pair of sandals.

By 6:15, we were in the Chevy and on the road to Edgartown. The clouds had gone away during the night and there were already some joggers trotting along the bike path and a quartet of clammers pulling on rake handles in Sengekontacket Pond even though the air was still cool from the night. I shivered at the thought of either running on hard blacktop or wading in 60-something-degree water at such an early hour.

"I don't dig that kind of vacation," Al said, pointing to the clam rakers, who were nearly up to their crotches in the water.

"I'd clam up about it if I were you," I said.

"Okay. I'll crawl back into my shell."

Edgartown's Main Street, which was usually clogged with barely-moving, bumper-to-bumper traffic, was almost empty. Parking places were plentiful, including several in the always-full tiny lot beside the harbor. We stopped behind the building that housed Henry Agnew's office, and Al stayed in the car while I walked around to the front door, hoping to be waiting there when Agnew arrived.

As expected, the door was locked, which meant I wouldn't have the pleasure of seeing the girl in the gold bikini. I turned toward the dock, where I saw the Krazy Karl and three smaller catamarans that looked like they'd each carry half a dozen people bobbing gently on the rippling water. There was a figure moving on the deck of the Krazy Karl, so I went through the passenger gate and walked down the ramp to the big boat. To my surprise, I saw that the figure was Henry Agnew.

He was dressed in washed-out blue jeans and an old gray T-shirt that hung halfway to his knees, and he was swabbing the deck, a chore I'd have expected to see a hired hand performing. He was concentrating so hard on the swirling mop that my cheery call of "good morning" startled him. He straightened up and stared at me a moment before returning the greeting with a noticeable lack of enthusiasm. "Can I help you?"

I stepped closer to the Krazy Karl. "Yes, you can," I said. "Remember me? Mitch Mitchell. We met last week at Harry

Dick's party out in Chilmark."

"Oh, yes. Aren't you one of the group that's staying with my old friend, Walt Jerome?"

"That's right; I'm one of the group. I've got some questions about our conversation that night and your secretary said this would be the best time of the day to talk to you."

"Oh?" Agnew said. "My secretary's not always correct. I'm really very busy right now, getting things ship-shape for the morning sails. Why don't you come back later? Take the sunset cruise and talk to me then."

"Actually, my questions won't take very long," I said. "Basically, I'm wondering why you lied to me."

That got his attention. He climbed down off the Krazy Karl onto the dock and stood facing me. "What the hell do you mean by that?" he asked.

"You told me that you'd only met the treasure hunter, Wade Waters, very briefly and hardly knew him, but I've learned that he was your business partner for a while before he left the island. Why did you lie about that?"

"Because I didn't think it was any of your goddamn business, that's why. Why are you poking around asking questions about Waters anyway?"

"I'm a writer," I said. "Stories about sunken treasure and murdered treasure hunters intrigue me."

"Well, tough shit," Agnew said. "Like I said, I'm very busy right now. And I'll probably be too busy to talk to you on the sunset cruise, so you might as well not come back. Have a good day." He turned away and took a step toward the Krazy Karl.

I pulled out the page I'd copied from the 10-year-old Gazette. "Stories like this also intrigue me," I said. "This headline says: 'Carly Smith engaged to Henry Agnew.' It's on an announcement that ran in the *Gazette* five months before Wayne Waters took off for Florida, accompanied by a woman named Carly Smith."

Agnew spun around faster than a dervish in the dunes. His face reddened and scrunched into a scowl. "So what if it did?"

"So it could explain why Wayne, later known as Wade, Waters was murdered when he returned to Oak Bluffs. The police might be quite interested in my suggestion of a possible connection."

I don't know where the gun came from. Agnew produced it so quickly that I didn't even see the move. What I did see was the business end of a snub-nosed .38 revolver pointing at my chest. This was a complication I had not foreseen, even though I should have, given my previous experience when accusing a man of murder on Martha's Vineyard.

"Okay, asshole, if you want to talk, let's go for a little boat ride and talk," Agnew said. He gestured toward the nearest small catamaran and told me to get on board. I obeyed and he followed.

The little cat was a basic model, with the mast at the forward edge of the platform connecting the twin hulls and a ship's wheel at the aft edge to control the rudder. In between were three rows of benches, each wide enough to seat four people. Under the middle bench was a crumpled blue plastic tarpaulin that appeared to have been stuffed into the opening between the bench's wooden legs.

The simple vessel could easily be sailed by two people and, in a pinch, by one. Although there would be two of us leaving the harbor, I had a feeling that Agnew planned on a solo return voyage. I wanted to yell for Al, but I was afraid the man with the gun would bring my backup buddy aboard as a second one-way traveler.

Agnew ordered me to sit on the deck forward of the wheel. I hunkered down between the twin hulls while, still keeping the gun pointed in my general direction, he released the fore and aft lines that secured the craft to the dock. With his free hand, he started the engine, took the wheel, maneuvered the cat into the harbor and steered toward the opening that led to the deeper waters of Nantucket Sound.

This was all too familiar. My previous trip to Martha's Vineyard had come to a climax aboard a power boat speeding across Nantucket Sound with a gun-toting killer at the throttle. I'd survived that adventure because Al had figured out where I was and summoned the harbor police. This time, I wasn't sure whether Al had moved into position to see my predicament or was still sitting fat, dumb and happy in the Chevy.

We passed the On Time Ferry landing, where the little barge sat waiting for its first run at 7 a.m., and the Edgartown lighthouse, where a lone photographer was walking in slow circles around the tower and shooting from every angle. Soon, we were in the sound and Agnew throttled back the engine to an idle so I could hear his voice. He ordered me to get up and hoist the sail, gesturing with the pistol toward which lines to pull and where to secure them.

When the sail was billowing in the wind, Agnew cut the engine. "So, ask your questions, Mr. Nosy Writer," he said. "I'll tell you anything you want to know now that you won't ever be able to write about it."

"All my friends know I came to talk to you this morning," I said. "They'll be looking for me at your dock." I opted not to mention the presence of Al in the parking lot, fearing it would inspire Agnew to shoot me before help hove into sight.

"Accidents happen," Agnew said. "It's a damn shame that you weren't wearing a life jacket when you fell overboard and hit your head. The Coast Guard will probably scold me for not forcing you to put one on. Might even fine me a hundred bucks. Don't you feel sorry for me?"

I choked back a sarcastic answer that might have provoked

him into pulling the trigger instantly because I needed to prolong the conversation. If Al had seen us board the cat, it would take several minutes for him to summon help. "Okay," I said. "Tell me all about what went on with you and Wade and Carly."

"What's to tell? The two-faced bitch admitted that she was screwing Waters the whole time she was engaged to me. When I caught them in the act, they laughed in my face and told me they were going off together. I'd have shot them both that night if I'd had a fucking gun."

"Why didn't you buy one and do it the next day?"

"I cooled off enough overnight to realize that I didn't want to spend the rest of my life in jail for killing two worthless pieces of shit," Agnew said. "Carly eventually got what she deserved in Florida when Wayne or Wade or whatever he was calling himself left her to drown."

"Do you think he could have saved her?"

"Of course he could have if he'd have been half awake. Stupid ass should never have let her go down. But, like I said, she got what she deserved."

"But you still wanted to get even with Waters when he came back to the Vineyard this spring?"

"Hell, yes. He'd run off with my fiancée and a boat that was half mine. And it was easy to set up that ignorant turd he brought back with him."

"You mean Morgan?" I asked.

"Of course, Morgan," Agnew said. "I've had my revenge and Morgan's on his way to life without parole." He turned the wheel a bit and our speed increased as a light following wind propelled the catamaran across the rippling waters of the sound toward the open sea.

"How'd you do it?" I was facing the stern and couldn't see any police boats pursuing us. "How'd you set Morgan up?"

"I called the idiot while he was sitting on his fat ass on the All That Glitters and said I was an old drinking buddy of his from New Bedford named Charlie. I figure you can find somebody named Charlie in every crappy, two-bit bar in New England, especially in a seaport. Morgan said he didn't remember drinking with any Charlie, but I named a couple of bars in New Bedford where creeps like him go to get shit-faced and he said okay, he'd meet me at the Gray Goose at 12:30 for a drink.

"While Morgan was in the Gray Goose waiting for Charlie, I was in the harbor tying a motor dinghy up to the stern of the All That Glitters. Then I climbed aboard and when Waters heard me walking around on deck, he came up from down below. I greeted him with this gun in one hand, hidden in my pants pocket so the people walking by wouldn't see it, and a baseball bat in the other.

"I made him take me out toward the spot where he was hunting for the shipwreck. I told him what an asshole he was, and he fell all over himself apologizing for taking off with Carly. Then I told him to get down on his knees and kiss my feet. He told me to kiss his ass and I smacked him in the face with the bat.

"He went down on his knees and I left the gun in my pocket and went to work on the bastard with the bat. He rolled onto his back and tried to protect himself with his arms but he didn't have prayer. After a few whacks, he managed to roll over and get onto his hands and knees, trying to get up and run, and that's when I nailed him on the back of the head. He flopped onto his belly and that was all she wrote. I checked for a pulse and there wasn't any.

"The next thing that happened was that the man fell overboard, sort of like you're going to do when we get out a little farther. Poor Wade or Wayne or whatever you want to put on his tombstone.

"Anyhow, it was the perfect set up. If the body never drifted in, I was home free. If the body was found, the coroner would find his skull cracked and call it homicide. The first suspect would be Morgan."

"And after dumping the body, you got into your dinghy and left the All That Glitters adrift?" I said.

"Exactly," Agnew said. "It was a nice calm day, like today, so getting back to Oak Bluffs in that little boat was a piece of cake." I was wishing for an even calmer day as we continued to cruise with the wind at our stern, speeding us toward wherever my ride was supposed to end.

One loose end remained untied in my mind. "I don't understand how Morgan could sit and wait in the bar where he was supposed to meet Charlie, but not be seen by either the bartender or the waitress who were working that day. He even claims he was served a beer."

"Another piece of cake. I own the Gray Goose and those two illegal immigrants from Brazil work for me. I told them what to say to the cops and warned them that I'd have them shipped back to where they came from if they didn't stick to the exact story that I gave them."

"You're very thorough," I said.

"That's why Wayne's in hell, Morgan's in jail and you're going swimming with the fishes," Agnew said. It seemed to me that the wind was picking up, sending us toward the open Atlantic at a faster clip. I still couldn't see any possible rescue boats behind us.

Finally, I stood up. Barely keeping my balance as the cat cut through the waves, I said, "There's no way I'm going over the side. You're going to have to shoot me, and there will be bullet wounds in my body when they find it."

Agnew laughed. "When they find it? Are you shittin' me? When I dump your body we'll be out where the current will take you to Greenland. That's if the sharks don't have you for dinner first."

I looked around the catamaran for some sort of shield. What I saw was not encouraging. If I ran toward the mast and ducked behind it before a bullet hit me, the darn thing wasn't thick enough to hide my entire body. He'd have a choice of taking target practice on either my gut or my butt. Likewise, diving onto a bench would be futile because Agnew could just walk over and plug me execution style.

My only chance for survival seemed to be a direct assault on the gunman. I gauged the distance between us and decided that I needed to creep a little closer before charging him. If I launched the attack from my current position he could probably put at least two bullets into me before I got to him. I slid my right foot forward, intending to attack his left side, where he was holding the wheel, and fell on my ass as the cat plowed into a wave.

"Thinking about trying to get to me before I can pull the trigger?" Agnew said. "Not a chance, landlubber. You can't even stand up long enough to take one step."

Dragging myself back onto my feet, I took a wide stance on the rocking deck and again calculated the time factor. The water was getting rougher as we neared the open sea and it seemed to be now or never.

"Come on, Mr. Nosy Writer, take a run at me," Agnew said. "I want to see how many slugs I can put in you before you hit the deck." He grinned, let go of the wheel, stepped to the side and took a two-handed grip on the pistol, the way the FBI guys do on the TV crime shows. "Nobody will ever know what happened to the great writer on his fatal catamaran ride."

"Except for me," said a loud voice from behind me and to my left.

CHAPTER 23

BATTLE AT SEA

Agnew's head swiveled toward the unseen speaker, and I charged full speed toward Agnew. I heard two shots fired and saw Agnew slump to the deck a second before I flung myself on top of him. The .38 was still clutched in his right hand and I concentrated on trying to pry it from his fingers, which left my crotch unprotected when he jammed his knee into my groin with enough force to blast away my breath and bring tears to my eyes.

I was still on top of Agnew but I was in helpless agony as he pulled his gun hand free of my limp fingers. Even the knowledge that the end of my life was just seconds away did not give me the strength to overcome the piercing pain in my groin and gut. With my eyes squinched tight shut, I lay sprawled across my would-be slayer waiting for an explosion from a gun muzzle inches from my head.

Instead of a shot, the next noise I heard was a foot smashing down on Agnew's hand, followed by the sound of his gun rattling loose on the deck. I opened my eyes in time to see the sneaker-shod foot kick the gun away from Agnew's groping fingers. The weapon was still spinning on the deck when a voice from above us ordered Agnew to stay down.

A rough hand gripped my shoulder and dragged me off of

Agnew's now motionless body. I curled into a fetal ball with both hands gripping the injured area, wishing my mother had never forced me out of that position and expelled me into the cruel world. My right cheek was pressing against a wet spot on the deck and, as the pain in my groin faded from unbearable to intense, I realized that the liquid under my face was blood.

When I rolled onto my back to get away from the blood, I got my first look at my rescuer. He was standing over me, with the kind of weapon the cops carry dangling loosely in his right hand.

"Family jewels all there?" asked Buck Studwell.

"I haven't taken inventory," I said in a gasping whisper, still gripping them with both hands. "How did you get here?"

"I been here all night," Buck said. "I rented this cat just before Natalie closed the office. I figured I could get an early start this morning if I slept onboard, so I crapped out on an air mattress under a tarp up forward under a seat. Hadn't planned on this early a start, though."

"You heard everything Agnew said?"

"Everything after the engine shut down. Lucky for both of us that he couldn't see me because I was wrapped up in the tarp."

"We're also lucky that you were quicker on the trigger."

"I wasn't taking any chances with that. I had him square in my sights before I yelled."

Still hurting, I dragged myself into a sitting position and looked at Agnew. He was on his back, with his left hand gripping his right side just above the waist. Blood was oozing between his fingers and running onto the deck to expand the puddle of red my face had lain in.

"I'd better turn this baby around," Buck said. He tucked the pistol into his belt, took the wheel and put the cat into a wide, sweeping 180-degree turn. "Hang on, Henry, old boy," he said to the cat's wounded owner. "We won't be moving quite so fast this direction. We're running almost dead against the wind."

The return trip to Edgartown was accomplished at half the speed we'd been traveling on our race toward the Atlantic. Along the way, Buck explained that he had rented the cat with the intention of sailing to the coordinates we'd decoded on Wade Waters's chart. "I wanted to check out the area before bringing out the boat with salvage gear," he said.

"I thought you were going to include at least one of your investors in your exploratory run," I said.

"I was planning to take Walt Jerome with me on a bigger boat next week sometime. You might say this was a preliminary to the preliminary."

I wasn't sure I believed him, but I wasn't complaining about his accompaniment on this particular trip. "Do you always pack a gun when you go sailing?" I asked.

"Only when there's a chance that I might meet somebody like the Bottoms Up crew out on the water. They could be out there looking for the wreck, you know."

I wondered how Dirk Oberman would feel if he learned that the possibility of his presence had saved my life. I decided to make a point of telling him if I had the misfortune of meeting him again.

We were within sight of the Cape Pogue lighthouse on Chappaquiddick when a Coast Guard cutter appeared off our starboard bow, closed rapidly and ordered us to heave to. After a sailor tossed us a line, they hauled us tight alongside and put a lieutenant with a sidearm and two enlisted men carrying rifles over as a boarding party.

"We got a call from the Edgartown Harbor Patrol saying they had an emergency out this way, but their boat was down with a bad engine," the lieutenant explained. "We were busy pulling out four people who were on a small boat that was hit broadside by some damn fool kid on a jet ski, so it took us a while to get over here. Hope everything's okay."

Buck pointed to the bleeding man on the deck and asked if the cutter had any medical personnel onboard. One of the enlisted boarders swung a small black bag off his back and announced that he was the ship's medic. He knelt beside Agnew and went to work with a syringe, compresses and tape. By the time we reached Edgartown harbor, Agnew was woozy from a painkiller and the wound was covered with a temporary bandage.

The Coast Guard cutter unleashed us when the lieutenant signaled that all was well, and we sailed onward and into Edgartown harbor with Buck Studwell at the helm. I was vertical but still tender in all the wrong places when we neared the dock and waved to a welcoming party that included Al, Dave, Walt, Carol, Cindy, four Edgartown police officers and an ambulance crew with a gurney.

I was greeted with hugs and kisses (the latter from the women only, thank heaven) and by an EMT who inquired about my physical condition. Buck Studwell was greeted by an officer who offered him a ride to the station to give a statement to the Edgartown police. Henry Agnew was greeted by two officers who placed him under arrest for kidnapping me and read him his Miranda rights. Then Agnew was loaded into an ambulance and driven away to the Martha's Vineyard Hospital in Oak Bluffs, escorted fore and aft by Edgartown PD cruisers.

"When no rescue boats showed up, I figured you hadn't seen Agnew force me onto the cat," I said to Al as we watched the array of blue and red flashing lights disappear.

"I kind of slid around the building and looked out just as the cat was beginning to move away from the dock," Al said. "I couldn't see you anywhere, but the guy at the wheel was holding something in his hand and I thought 'here we go again.' I called the harbor patrol right away, told them you'd been taken out of the harbor at gunpoint and damn near shit my shorts when they said their boat was down for repairs. They said they'd call the Coast Guard, but I was scared they'd never get to you in time."

"They didn't," I said. "If Buck hadn't decided to sleep on the cat he'd rented, I'd be sleeping with the sharks in the Atlantic right now."

"Saved from an eternal snooze in the seabed," Al said.

"No water bed for Mitch," Dave said.

"And no more bullshit from you about a vacation I'll never forget," I said.

"Hey, I bet you won't ever forget it," Dave said. "And I never did say why you wouldn't."

"And think how your adventure on the water will pump up that story you've been writing," Al said. "You can send it to a dozen magazines and the offers will come pouring in."

"Oh, sure," I said. "And while offers are pouring in, can you imagine the profanity that will be pouring out of our city editor if the *Daily Dispatch* doesn't get my first-person version before it's sold to anyone else?"

"That's true," Al said. "You'd probably be better off playing with the sharks than pissing off Don O'Rourke."

I said goodbye to the Coast Guardsmen, who were waiting for transportation back to their station at Menemsha, and started walking toward the Chevy with Al and Carol.

Carol noticed that I was bending slightly forward and taking short steps. "What's wrong, Mitch?" she asked. "Did you hurt your legs?"

"I'd rather not discuss what part of me got hurt," I said. "Let's just say it's an egregious flesh wound."

Carol smiled. "I think I understand. Maybe it should be looked at."

"Who'd want to look at it?" I asked.

"Well, I expect that Martha will when she comes home, but for the moment, I was thinking of someone in the medical profession. I'm sure you don't want the flesh to be weak the next time the will is strong."

She would mention Martha. Now I was hurting emotionally as well as physically. Where was Martha? Why didn't she call? Would she ever care about the strength of that particular piece of my flesh again?

"The flesh will heal without the help of a doctor," I said. I wasn't so sure about repairing the emotional damage if I didn't hear from Martha very soon.

At the request of still another officer, we made a side trip to the Edgartown police station, where I perched on the edge of a wooden chair, answered a long list of questions posed by a detective and wrote a description of my ordeal. I detected the flicker of a smile when he reached the paragraph about my injury, but he made no comment. I wondered if he was naturally reticent about discussing highly personal issues, as many New Englanders are, or if he'd been given special sensitivity training.

"We might need to talk to you again," he said when he finished reading and looked up.

"Any time," I said. I didn't tell him that I'd be flying back to St. Paul in less than 24 hours. No need to cause him concern.

When we got back to the cottage, I climbed the stairs at half-speed, one step at a time, went to my bedroom, surprised Sherlock Holmes with a hug and released my cell phone from its overnight port of restoration on the charger. It was late Saturday afternoon in Cape Verde and the attorney general's office was closed, but I called the number anyway on the off chance that Martha might be working overtime on a difficult case. Again, I was shunted to her voice mail. This time, I didn't bother leaving a message.

I went gingerly down the stairs, walked slowly out to the porch and found my five housemates preparing lunch. Suddenly, I was ravenously hungry. It was almost 1 p.m., and I'd been up for nearly seven hours, during which I had endured a nerve-wracking boat ride, a savage assault on the tenderest area of my body and a lengthy grilling by an unsympathetic detective, all without sustenance of any sort.

Carol waved me toward a chair with a cushion. "What can I make for the wounded hero?" she asked.

"Right now, I could eat half a cow, but I'll settle for about a pound of rosemary ham between two slices of bread," I said.

"Do you want fries with that?" she asked.

"How about a couple bags of chips?"

"There's only half a bag left, but it's all yours," she said, handing it to me. They were sour cream and garlic flavored, which is not on my list of favorites, but I started stuffing handfuls of chips into my mouth while Carol stacked a mound of ham on a slice of rye bread, added two slices of deli cheese, spread mustard on another slice of rye, put it all together and handed to me. It was the best meal I'd had since the finish of my Navy survival training, when our bedraggled crew of survivors received an air-drop of canned beans and wieners after three days of living on sea cucumbers, shellfish the size of my thumbnail and juice squeezed from thorny cactus leaves.

I was chewing the last bite of ham and thinking about seconds when a rusty pickup truck rattled to a stop in front of the cottage. Detective Gouveia emerged, came to the bottom of the porch steps and pointed at me. "I need you to come down to the station with me," he said. "The chief just heard about your latest boat ride from the Edgartown PD and I've gotta take a statement from you before we can do anything about releasin' your buddy, Captain Morgan." The tone with which he pronounced "Captain" did not indicate respect for the man's self-acclaimed rank.

"Can't you take a statement here?" I asked, not wishing to be bounced around in Gouveia's beat-up jalopy.

"Department procedure requires that I do it at the station. Don't worry, I'll get you back in time to go to the beach."

"That's the least of my worries," I said, rising slowly from the chair.

"Take the cushion with you," Al said.

"Good idea." I picked the pad up off the chair and walked cautiously down the porch steps.

"What happened?" Gouveia asked. "Hurt your legs wrestlin' with the gunslinger?"

"I'm not required by department procedure to discuss the cause and nature of my injury until we get to the station. Just try not to hit any big potholes or speed bumps, okay?"

Gouveia grinned. "Got'cha in the nuts, did he?"

I maintained a dignified silence as I placed the cushion on the seat and slid gently onto it. Gouveia was still grinning as he started the engine, but he did drive carefully, avoiding a couple of major potholes on the way to the station.

"What Buck Studwell and I heard from Agnew and told to the Edgartown cops should exonerate Morgan," I said. "Why do you need another statement from me?"

"Because Morgan's officially our prisoner, not Edgartown's," Gouveia said. "We need statements from you and Studwell before the DA can go into court and ask for Morgan's release."

"Will he be out today?"

"No way. The judge is off-island for the weekend. Morgan will remain as a guest of the public at least 'til Monday."

"I guess he won't be dropping by the cottage to thank me then," I said.

"Are you shittin' me?" Gouveia said. "If that sleaze bag was let out of the can right now, he wouldn't walk across the sidewalk to say thanks, so don't expect no cards in the mail."

"Very poor manners, I must say."

"Poor manners is the least of that asshole's problems."

"How so?"

"He's gonna have to fight it out with Studwell for part ownership of the All That Glitters and for his right, if any, to a share of whatever comes up from the Daniel French," Gouveia said. "Not to mention competition from the Bottoms Up, which is still out there lookin' for the wreck. They went out before sunup this mornin', as a matter of fact." I thought about Buck Studwell packing a gun in case the Bottoms Up was on the scene and didn't know whether to be concerned or grateful.

"The six of us are all supposed to get a percentage of what Studwell salvages from the Daniel French," I said. "Sounds like we might have to wait quite awhile to collect it."

"I wouldn't spend my millions before I saw them if I was you. By the time they decide who owns what, you could be drawin' Social Security."

"Oh, damn. I was planning to use my share to buy a five-million-dollar house on Ocean Park, overlooking the Oak Bluffs police station."

Gouveia was grinning again. "No shit? I thought you'd be buyin' a boat so's you could run around on Nantucket Sound for old time's sake."

"If I never ride on any water craft smaller than the ferry to Woods Hole again it will be too damn soon," I said.

CHAPTER 24

THE GETAWAY

It took me about an hour and a half to answer Gouveia's questions and write out what I hoped was the same statement I'd authored in Edgartown. The detective drove me back to Walt Jerome's cottage, again taking care to avoid major jolts.

"We'll be out of here early tomorrow," I said as I slid out of the pickup. "We're busing it to Logan and catching a 1:20 flight, so I guess this is goodbye."

"Well, thanks for doin' my job for me," the detective said. "I should have thought about lookin' at Agnew for the murder, knowin' the history of those two guys and the woman, but Morgan was such an easy target. Anyhow, drop in the next time you're on the Vineyard."

"Nothing personal, but I hope I never see the Vineyard again," I said. "Two boat rides at gunpoint are enough."

"It ain't always like that. Millions of people who come here never see the barrel of a gun."

"I seem to attract the minority of islanders who do have guns, so I'm staying away forever. So long, detective."

"You'll come back," Gouveia said with a wave of his hand. "Everybody does."

No way in hell, I thought as I climbed the stairs to the porch.

My five companions were sitting there, all wearing swim suits.

"Last chance for the beach," Dave said. "Get your suit on and let's go. We'll let you ride in the Chevy because it's got better springs than the Land Rover."

"I wasn't aware that the Land Rover had any springs at all," I said.

"Its springs have been sprung," Dave said. "Hurry up while there's some sunshine left."

"I'm not in condition to hurry either up or down, but I'll change as quick as I can without maximum discomfort."

"Okay. We'll make allowance for your delicate condition. Would you like someone to help you change?"

"Yes, if you've got someone about 22 years old whose picture has appeared recently in the centerfold of *Playboy*," I said.

"We were thinking of someone more local, like Daffy Dolly," Al said.

"That's not only local, it's loco," I said. "I'll be down in whatever time it takes to ease my injured parts into a swimsuit, unassisted, thank you very much."

"We'll be waiting at this location," Al said. He always has to have the last word.

We did the beach thing, with me lying on a blanket on the softest available sand while the others got all wet and salty. Later, after our showers, we celebrated our final night with Walt by taking him to dinner at a high-buck restaurant in Edgartown. The food was no better than what we'd had at our favorite haunt in Oak Bluffs, but the surroundings were more panache and my friends were able to wash down their various orders of sea scallops, swordfish and clams with a fine, and exceedingly expensive, white wine, which wasn't available at Linda Jean's. I settled for coffee with my broiled bluefish, which I ordered for my final Vineyard dinner because it wouldn't be available back in Minnesota.

★ ★ ★

I'd like to report that our departure on Sunday morning was pleasant and routine. Unfortunately, I cannot. I awoke to the sound of rain hammering against the window (and spraying in through the gap I'd left open for the passage of fresh air while I slept). After closing the window, I dressed in jeans and a short-sleeved sport shirt for the trip to Boston's Logan International Airport, fed Sherlock Holmes in the kitchen and fought him into his traveling cage. The carrier was not popular with Sherlock because its most frequent use involved visits to the vet.

The rain continued, varying in intensity between downpour and deluge. The ferry we needed to catch in order to make our bus and airline connections was leaving from Vineyard Haven, some three miles away. Our combined luggage, including Sherlock's cage, was too much to cram into the old Chevy's trunk, so Walt wound up driving us to the ferry landing in two shifts.

We said our hasty thank you's and goodbyes in the car before grabbing our gear out of the trunk and running through the rain to the shelter of the terminal. Fortunately for me, the ache and soreness in my groin had been reduced overnight to a bearable state of tenderness, and I was able to move at almost top speed.

We watched from the terminal while a huge white ferry called Island Home pulled into the slip and the cars and passengers disembarked in the downpour. It being Martha's Vineyard, the torrential rain was routinely accompanied by a stiff northeast wind. The wind velocity was far short of what Al and I had experienced during the storm in our previous visit, but it was strong enough to provide us with a source of entertainment. We were able to amuse ourselves by counting the number of umbrellas that were turned inside out and reduced to trash after being popped open by optimistic passengers proceeding down the gangway.

When the bumbershoot demolition derby ended, it was our turn to make the move through the rain to the gangway and up to the ferry. We gathered our gear and splashed across the wide stretch of watery blacktop, along with a hundred others, to the metal gangway, which was slick with running water. We didn't have to pause to have our tickets torn in two because the ticket tearer had taken shelter just inside the ferry entrance instead of manning his usual station at the foot of the ramp. However, a woman in front of me slipped to her hands and knees and I chose to stop long enough for her to regain her feet instead of running over her back. This exposed me to an additional 30 seconds of rainfall, which meant I was drenched instead of merely soaked by the time I ducked through the ferry entrance.

Fortunately, the Island Home is a huge boat with a large inside seating capacity, and the early-morning run is not a popular departure time, because the outside seats were unusable in the wind and rain. Unfortunately, a number of passengers were accompanied by dogs and the smell of wet canine soon became pervasive throughout the ferry. Apparently this odor upset Sherlock Holmes, because he began to yowl like a scalded banshee and I couldn't persuade him to shut up. I finally set his cage outside on the deck, close to the bulkhead and under a small overhang.

Because of the wind, the water was choppy and the ride was unusually rough. *What a perfect departure from an island that seemed to want me dead*, I thought. The wind-driven rain followed us across the sound and slanted into our faces at a slightly-reduced but steady rate when we disembarked in Woods Hole. This meant splashing through a hundred yards of puddles to reach the Bonanza Bus, which stood idling and spewing exhaust on the far side of the parking lot.

Upon arriving at Logan and checking in with Northwest Airlines, we learned that our flight was delayed indefinitely because of the storm, which had engulfed the entire east coast and fouled up flights from Atlanta, Georgia, all the way to Augusta, Maine. We hung out in the various airport shops, trying to dry out and snacking on overpriced food until our flight was finally called at a few minutes after 3.

Again, I went through the airport routine with Sherlock Holmes. First the security people insisted that he should be checked baggage and yielded with great reluctance when I showed them the boarding pass and asked them to summon a supervisor. Then the woman scanning boarding passes at the gate informed me in her most authoritative, school-marm voice that I could only take one carry-on bag aboard the aircraft.

"This one has a ticket," I said, holding the cat carrier up in front of her face. "Would you like me to check the carrier and see how long the puddy-tat will stay in his assigned seat without it?" The woman leaned forward until her nose nearly touched the carrier to peek in and Sherlock hissed at her. She jerked her head back so fast I was afraid that she'd have whiplash and waved me through to the boarding ramp.

I had the window seat and Sherlock was parked in the center seat between me and a puffy-faced, coat-and-tied salesman type who looked like he wanted to chat. Chatting was not on my agenda, and I avoided eye contact by alternately staring out the window and burying my nose in a paperback edition of the latest adventure of a crime-solving cat called Midnight Louie. Sometimes I entertain Sherlock Holmes with the parts allegedly written by the cat, but this was neither the time nor place for reading aloud.

While staring and burying, I mostly was thinking about Martha. Where had she gone? Why wasn't she returning my calls and e-mails? Was I about to lose another woman I loved?

Mentally, I ran through my life list of lovers. First there was tall, blond Karen Langley, whom I'd married when I was a Navy ensign in Pensacola, Florida, and lost—along with our two-week-old son—in a head on crash with a semi-trailer in Alameda, California.

Next in line was short, curly-haired Jennifer Tilton, who left me to go live with her high school sweetheart in New Jersey the day I was going to propose marriage to her in Minnesota.

Then came gorgeous, brown-skinned Martha Todd, who I met soon after she'd divorced an abusive husband and begun studying to become a lawyer. Both of us were afraid of emotional commitment during the early part of our relationship, and when we finally broke the barrier more than a year later, it was almost time for her to fulfill her scholarship contract in Cape Verde.

During the first half of Martha's three-year absence, I was comforted by the Rev. Margaret Hayes, a slender, blue-eyed Unitarian Universalist minister who could have been the love of my life if I hadn't given my heart to Martha. Margaret left the church in Minnesota's St. Croix Valley to take over the pulpit of a larger church in her native Massachusetts. Since Margaret's departure, I had been struggling to avoid sexual entanglements that could complicate my life upon Martha's return, hence my interminable angst about a potential romp in a dark bedroom with the luscious Rhonda Fairchild.

If funks really were blue, I'd have been swathed in the color of a Marine's dress uniform when our plane touched the runway in Minnesota shortly after suppertime. The others were pleased to see that it wasn't raining, but I didn't give a damn what the weather was doing as long as we were home. Somewhere among the jetsam I'd collected during my last visit to Cape Verde was a card bearing the name and office phone number of Martha's supervisor. Tomorrow I would get up at 4 a.m. and call the man to ask him where she was.

We were all still damp when we squeezed into a three-seat taxi at the terminal, so we decided to go our separate ways for the evening meal rather than invade a restaurant wearing wet-smelling clothing and lugging an unhappy cat in a carrier.

Dave and Cindy bailed out at their home on Edgcumbe Road, where they were greeted on the front steps by their two teenage daughters and Cindy's mother, who had been staying with the girls as part cook and part party-discourager.

Al and Carol, whose kids had been boarded out, invited me to share whatever they could find in their kitchen. Sixteen-year-old Kristin, who was the city's top teenage softball pitcher, was staying with her coach, Heather Layne, because the girls' summer season was at its competitive peak. Kevin, 14, who loved to fish with grandpa, was staying with Carol's parents near Mille Lacs.

I thanked Carol for the offer and opted for my own apartment even though I knew the cupboard was bare. I was in no mood to be sociable, even with my best friends. My plan was to phone for a large pepperoni-and-mushroom pizza and take a hot shower while waiting for delivery. After sharing the pizza with Sherlock and watching the 10 p.m. news, I would go to bed grumpy.

When the taxi stopped in front of my building on Grand Avenue, I paid my share of the tab and tip, said "so long" to Al and Carol, and went in towing my suitcase in my right hand and lugging Sherlock's carrier and my laptop in the other. I let go of the suitcase handle in front of my apartment door and fished the key out of my pocket. To my amazement, the door swung open while I was pushing the key into the lock.

"It's about time you got here," said a familiar female voice. There in the open doorway stood the most beautiful woman in the world, Martha Todd, with her incredibly white smile glowing, her jet black curls framing her round, coffee-with-cream-complexioned face and her deep green eyes sparkling with mischief. Beneath the gorgeous face, encased in skin-tight blue jeans and a Minnesota Twins T-shirt, was the body that I loved to hold tight against mine.

Stunned speechless, I dropped the laptop and poor Sherlock with a crash, bringing forth a yowl of complaint from inside the cat carrier.

"I've been waiting here for almost a week," Martha said. "And look who I brought back with me." She took a step backward and a tall, dark-skinned, young man stepped up beside her.

"Hey, Mitch," the tall, dark-skinned, young man said. "Remember me? Frederico Lopes."

My knees turned to overcooked spaghetti and I was forced to grab the door jamb to keep from falling on my face.

CHAPTER 25

WELCOME HOME

Apparently my face also mimicked spaghetti by turning the color of uncooked angel hair underneath my Vineyard suntan. Martha grabbed me by the shoulders and steered me toward a kitchen chair, where she sat me down and asked, "Are you okay, Hon?"

"I'm fine," I lied. "Just a little woozy from the trip, I guess. You know, jet lag and all that kind of stuff."

"You looked like you were about to faint," she said. "Sit there and I'll get you some water."

While Martha was filling a glass from the kitchen faucet and I was taking some deep breaths, Frederico dragged my suitcase, the laptop and the cat carrier inside and shut the door. I accepted the water glass, took a long swig and said, "Why don't you say hi to Sherlock?"

Martha opened the carrier and Sherlock bounded out. Without breaking stride, he dashed out of the kitchen and into the living room on his way to his usual haunt, my bedroom. Halfway through the living room he slammed on the brakes, turned his head and looked back. Seeing Martha, the cat raced back to the kitchen and practically leaped into her arms. *Lucky Sherlock*, I thought. *That's where I should be.*

Frederico strolled to my chair and leaned over me. "You feeling okay now, Mitch old man?"

"I'm fine," I said, standing up and forcing him to retreat a step. *Old man*, indeed! Unfortunately, my legs were still so wobbly that I had to make a quick grab for the back of the chair, which took some of the pizzazz out of my recovery.

"Well, I'll be heading back to my place then," Frederico said. "See you guys tomorrow, maybe?"

"Your place?" I asked.

"Yeah. I got an apartment over in Minneapolis. You don't think I been staying here with your lady, do you?"

"Oh, no. Never." I almost flopped into the chair again as my knees began to buckle from relief.

"My god, Mitch, don't pass out," Martha said. "I wanted to surprise you; I didn't mean to give you a heart attack."

"You did really good with your surprise," I said. "I wasn't expecting to see you home until November."

"They let me go a couple months early because they had some new blood coming in fresh out of school," she said. "I made the people in the office promise not to tell you I was on the way to St. Paul."

"What about your buddy here?" I asked.

"Frederico landed a job with a law firm in downtown Minneapolis," Martha said. "He's been wanting to come to the United States, and I knew some people who could help him find a place to work."

"That's great," I said, trying to sound like I meant it. My fear was that she might have found a job in the same office.

Martha must have read my mind. "I'm hooking up with the firm out in Highland Park where I clerked while I was going through law school," she said. "I had it wired before we left Cape Verde."

"That's great," I said again. This time I really meant it.

"Well, I'm gone, guys," Frederico said. "Have a good night." As he went out the door, he turned back and gave me a look that indicated he knew what kind of activity I had in mind for making the night good.

Frederico closed the door softly behind him. Martha and I stood a few feet apart, facing each other.

"You must be starved," Martha said.

"I'm famished," I said, stepping toward her.

"Me, too," she said, draping her arms around my neck. We had most of our clothes off by the time we reached the bedroom.

The End